Wave Song

A DEEP WATERS NOVELLA

EMMA HAMM

For everyone who saw a merman romance where he has two dicks and thought "I'll give it a shot".
And then got surprised with a slowburn.

CHAPTER
One

THE SEA BREEZE tangled in Aly Fairweather's hair, toying with the blonde ends and sweeping them into her face. Waves crashed against the sides of her submarine, one of the first designed by her father, and even though some of the salty water slid inside the vessel, she wasn't worried. Alys Fairweather had never been afraid of the sea.

Storms gathered on the horizon, their black clouds tangling around each other. This storm would glide past without bothering her, but she knew that within were icy shards of hail the size of daggers. There was a town in that direction, and it would likely be destroyed by the high winds and the massive ice clumps that ripped through any building.

The land was soon to be uninhabitable. If it wasn't the hurricanes, the ice storms, or the insanely high winds, it was the earthquakes that rumbled beneath the sea and stirred up massive tsunamis that swept entire cities back with it.

But she had never been all that afraid. Life was too exciting to live on its own, why should she be terrified of the unknown? Or perhaps that was her father's wild spirit inside her.

After all, he was one of the greatest engineers alive.

Her father had sent her out on this mission on her own. As

this was the first time she'd ever piloted a sub without his careful gaze upon her, she knew this was an important mission to do well. If she was lucky, then she'd be the person to scout out the next area for their cities to be built.

Shielding her eyes from the sun, she glanced back at the mountain that had already spewed lava from its top. The volcanos were angry today, and soon the sky would be swallowed by dark ash. It was best if she got back underneath the water.

And yet...

She watched the billowing cloud extend toward her through the air. The madness of excitement coursed through her veins and she stood there, staring down death itself for a few more moments before disappearing into the sub. The top clanged shut behind her, and a small giggle of elation escaped her lips.

She shouldn't toy with nature like that. Her father would be horrified to know she was taking so many risks when he had taught her to be careful in every way possible. Especially under the sea.

There were always rules to follow. Only use one third of an oxygen tank before turning around. Check every possible part of the ship before getting in it. Never stare too long into the abyss.

Sliding into her seat, she buckled herself in as the world went dark. Volcanic ash blocked the sun completely, which meant soon the water temperatures around her would rise.

The sharp click of her seatbelt echoed in the small sub. It was little more than a bubble. Just a circle that was filled with endless equipment and tools. There were hundreds of buttons on the walls, gauges and meters for every possible element she could control.

The front of the sub was made out of very thick glass. And the entirety of the ocean was laid out before her, like there was nothing standing in her way. She was in a pristine submarine that was made to survive almost any circumstance. Other than a small chip on the top right of the circular dome, but that had been a mistake when she'd been first learning how to drive this.

She was better now. And certainly didn't run into that many rocks.

Grabbing the two control sticks in front of her, one for speed and one for direction, she plunged into the darkness of the sea. The lights on the front of her submarine helped guide her sometimes, but most of the time, it was just pure darkness down here.

Those were her favorite spots. The depths called to some part of her soul that yearned for the sharp edge of fear and excitement. Her father always scolded her about it, saying that she was a reckless young woman who would find herself sunk at the bottom of the sea if she wasn't careful. But she lived for moments when all the world fell away and it was just her and the ocean.

Sometimes she got lucky, and there were deep-sea creatures that appeared in her lights. Giant squid. Whales. Strange fish with lights attached to their heads or bioluminescent bodies that glowed the moment they realized there could be a predator in their midst. There was no color in the depths, because all light was swallowed by the beating heart of the sea.

But today was not one of those days. She couldn't go into the deep just to test the structural integrity of her ship. She had to zip through the waters, farther and farther away from what she knew to be her home.

Leaning forward, she flicked a red switch that opened up the communication channel with her favorite droid friend. Her father had created it as a companion for her long ago, even though the droid did have a designation and a duty. But mostly, its duty was to keep her company. "Hello there, Beta Epsilon Iota."

"Good morning, Alys."

"Is it morning still?" She twisted one of the controllers, curving the sub around a pillar of stone, perhaps a little too quickly. A few panels in front of her flashed red, then calmed back down once she righted the sub.

"Your father has always said you are reckless in steering," the droid grumbled. "I am certain anyone else would also agree with him."

"I'm not reckless," she said with a laugh, tilting the sub at another dangerous angle that flashed more red throughout the inner pod. "I'm just faster than other people. I know the limits of the machine."

"And how much whale oil is left?"

Alys wasn't sure about that. There were solar panels on the top of the sub that she usually relied on if she ran out of fuel. Of course... There was no sun today.

"Damn it," she muttered. "How much farther do I have?"

"Approximately three miles."

"And how far are we from Alpha?"

The droid paused for dramatics. "Sixteen."

She dropped her hands from the controllers and let the sub slow to a halt. "Fuck."

"That is not a lady-like word."

"Beta..." She squeezed her eyes shut and reminded herself that the droid was here to help her. "Why didn't you tell me this sooner?"

"It's your mission. I am not to interfere."

She was going to open the panel the droid was stored in and rip it out. Beta knew better than to anger her, and some part of her whispered to toss it into the open water. Just for a few moments. Not forever. Only long enough to give the droid a good scare before taking it back into her ship.

But then she would be alone in the ocean, and she wasn't certain she wanted to deal with that either. Sighing, she thumped her head against the back of the stiff seat. "So, what do you suggest?"

"Charging the batteries with solar energy, while we use the rest of the whale oil to maintain life support."

"Right." That was the logical step. Not to push her luck and see just how far she could go before the air started getting really thin.

Narrowing her eyes, she leaned forward to guide them to a spot that was a little more safe. It wasn't that she was reckless or too young to be doing this. Alys just lived a very quiet life outside of this submarine and every time she got in it she got a little... well. Reckless.

Soon enough, she found soft sand to put the submarine down in. There was a small kelp forest nearby, and they were close enough to the surface for the sun's rays to reach her ship, and also for her to swim up if life support went down. At the very least, she could breathe ashy air for a while and tread water.

Maybe Beta realized what she was doing. "You can't breathe the air up there, Alys. It will burn your lungs."

"Better a good lung burning than dying without oxygen down here." Unbuckling herself, she leaned the chair back so she could at least relax while she was down here.

Besides, she had the best view on the planet right now.

It took a while, but that wasn't really surprising. The sub landing had stirred up dust and sand, so it was hard to see them, anyway. The creatures of the sea always hid at the arrival of some kind of giant creature in their midst.

Soon, creatures bloomed like flowers. First, it was the schools of fish, those who were used to larger animals in their midst. Bright emeralds and flickering yellows that speckled throughout the waves and turned to gemstones in any light that caught on them. Then the crustaceans dug out of the sand where they had hid, returning to finding their food in the thin dust and sand. Their shells were dotted with blue tinged spikes and the tips of their claws were ombre teal. Then a few turtles even swam before the lights of her submarine.

Her attention caught on the small schools of brightly colored fish that swam through the kelp. A seal turned to look at her, those big black eyes seeing so much. She scooted closer to watch all the plants and animals burst to life. Could flesh this out more with colors of coral or the sun filtering through the water etc.

Beta clinked in its panel. "You should turn the lights off, Miss Alys. You're wasting energy."

"You want me to sit in the dark until the ash lets the sunlight through?" she snorted. "I'm not going to miss a second of this."

The ash would eventually settle. She had Beta send a message to her father to let him know she had gotten stuck, but that she'd return once the sub charged up again. It must not have been too much of a surprise for her father, because he didn't reply with anything other than a single word.

"Okay."

No one could say her father didn't trust her, at least.

She must have dozed off for a little while, because the lights were off when she snapped back awake. Alys shook her head, blinking the grit out of her eyes as she tried to figure out why she had woken at all.

Rubbing the headache between her eyes, she sat up and let her boots thud onto the floor. Her pants were wet, somehow. And when she looked up, she could see the hatch was dripping in the dim blue interior lights. Damn it. A leak?

"The last thing I need," she muttered, standing up to press her finger against the leak. Not a bad one, by any means. But it did mean the hull wasn't as sturdy as she'd originally thought.

This was fine. She could fix this. They had a welder in here somewhere, and if she had to seal herself inside the sub until she could get home, then that was fine.

"Beta?" she asked, turning to rummage through one of the storage containers. "Do you know where I put the welder?"

"Miss Alys, I don't think we're alone anymore."

"Very funny. Did Dad send someone to find me, after all?" She yanked out what felt like a welder, but ended up being the broken end of a screwdriver. "Damn it."

"Alys!" Beta's voice was a little harsher this time. "Turn around."

Sighing, she had a whole rant on the tip of her tongue to scold the droid for trying to scare her, but then all the words disappeared the moment the droid turned on the lights outside of the pod.

A man floated outside of her sub.

No, not a man.

Something else entirely.

His long, dark hair hovered around his head, graceful and delicate in comparison to the hard swath of muscles that tapered down from his broad shoulders to a very narrow waist. But that was all that looked human. She could see the delicate webs between his fingers that ended in deadly black claws. The gills that fluttered on the side of his neck and the bright green scales that created a tiger stripe pattern all down his body. It was...

What was he?

"Beta," she whispered. "Have we documented any creatures such as this?"

"No."

So she was the first.

His eyes followed her movement as she approached the glass. Startlingly, they were entirely black. Not a single hint of white or color at all. Just pitch black, demon eyes. But she couldn't find it in herself to be frightened of this creature on the other side of her submarine. Even though she knew the leak in the hull had compromised the structural integrity.

She'd seen nothing like him before, and that made her heart thunder in her chest. She wanted to talk to him, to touch him. To do anything that would make him seem more real.

"My father used to tell me stories about the people who lived in the sea," she whispered, drawing ever closer to the glass. "He said the women were so beautiful it made your eyes hurt to look at them. I didn't realize it would extend to the men as well."

"Creatures?" Beta asked, flicking a few more of the exterior lights on. "What kind of creatures?"

"Undines," she replied. "At least, that's what the myths

called them. They were men and women who lived under the water, stealing sailors away from their family to lock them away in underwater cities."

"Please tell me you're not entertaining that thought," Beta grumbled.

She was.

Oh, she absolutely was.

Finally, she was right in front of the glass. Leaning over the console so there was just a thick layer of protection from him. If he came any closer, she'd been able to count the scales that dotted down his sides and lingered around his ribs. She might even be able to see how many layers of gills fluttered down his neck and connected to his ears.

He floated closer, flicking a massive tail that she realized actually went around her ship. A faint tapping from above had her turning her gaze up to see the faint outline of his tail that draped over the top of her submarine.

"Wow," she whispered. "You're massive, aren't you?"

The diamond shaped tail tapped again, and she reached out her hand to touch the glass underneath it. Though it flinched the moment she reached for it, eventually the tail laid flat. She couldn't touch it, or feel it, but she could see the powerful muscles and the delicate veins that spider-webbed through it.

The undine, as she was calling it, had used this opportunity to come ever closer to her. By the time she turned her attention back to him, she realized he was right there. So close she could have touched him if there wasn't glass between them.

Her lips parted on a gasp as she stared into those black eyes. He didn't seem to want to hurt her. In fact, she would hazard a guess that he was just as interested in her as she was him. His gaze was filled with curiosity, not hatred like she might expect. He was interested in her, or at least in her existence.

Carefully, slowly, the creature lifted his hand and pressed it against the glass of the submarine. His hand was as large as her head, huge and foreboding, with those giant claws at the end of it. If he wanted to rip into her, he easily could. He could tear her into little pieces and then leave her to bleed out in the ocean.

But she didn't think he would. It was a deep, gut feeling that he didn't want to harm her. He just wanted to know what she was.

Reaching out, she mirrored his movement and laid her hand against his palm. Though the glass was cool, she could almost imagine the texture of his skin and the smoothness of those webs. He was... Everything.. Strange. Unusual. Beautiful.

A creature no one in her world had ever seen before.

"Who are you?" she whispered, freezing when his gaze locked on her lips. "Do you speak?"

He opened his mouth and let out a sound like the song of a whale. Long and low, it vibrated through the very glass and settled deep into her bones. The sound was so soothing, it immediately relaxed any tense muscles in her body. This strange creature was more attractive than any man she'd ever met.

Maybe it was because he was new. Maybe it was because she'd never thought to see a creature appear out of a fairytale. Or maybe it was simply the deep hollows between his abs and the strong shoulders that flexed underneath her gaze. She didn't know.

What Alys did know was that she wanted this creature. More than she'd ever wanted any other man.

Licking her lips, she tried to get control over her emotions by saying, "My name is Alys. What's yours?"

The ship flickered, lights coming back on. Red panels started blinking all over and the ship itself gave a rumble as the power turned back on.

The undine in front of her bared his teeth, the expression a sudden flash of sharp edges and flesh tearing fangs before he darted away from the ship. That massive, powerful tail sent him careening away from Alys and into the kelp forest; disappearing all in the span of one breath.

Her knees wobbled, and suddenly Alys realized she was

rather shaky. Every part of her body quivered as she slumped into her seat and blew out a long breath. "Beta?"

"Alys?"

"What's the report?"

"Most of the systems are offline, but if you activate the emergency protocol, it will bring us back to the base while maintaining life support."

"Okay." Her eyes stayed glued to the glass and the spot where the undine had disappeared. "Activate emergency protocol."

CHAPTER
Two

FLICKING HIS TAIL, Imber darted through the waves and crested the surface. Flinging himself into the warm air, he rotated mid leap before splashing back into the waves again. There was much to celebrate today. Namely, his sister was to become a mother. Already, the entire pod was waiting with her. They gathered around the beauty of her extended belly and sang the songs of the ancients.

She would continue their bloodline with her birth. A miraculous thing, considering she was the only sister he had. Imber had come from a smaller family. His mother had difficulty with each pregnancy, and she'd only had the two of them survive. So to see his line continue in his sister's name? Ah, it made his entire body feel light.

Males were not allowed to attend the ceremony, of course. This was women's work, and the matriarch would allow them to see the babe when she was ready. And when his sister was ready too, of course.

He just... He couldn't wait to see the new life. It had been a long time since his pod had a child to dote on, and now they would all have a new baby to spoil rotten.

Perhaps he would bring the child a seashell from the far off hunting grounds. If his lovely sister had a daughter, then they would need abalone to create the perfect comb for her hair.

But, as was often these days, any time his mind went to adventure, it also went to the new creature he had discovered only a week ago.

A woman, he reminded himself. It had spoken.

They'd seen her kind before. The achromos, they called them. Because all the creatures that came into their sea were so... colorless as she had been. Pale skin, pale eyes, pale hair. There was nothing on her body that even suggested she had color at all. Just like the inside of a clam. Disgusting, really, but he had found this one rather... pretty.

In her own way, of course. She wasn't the beauty like the large females of their pod. He was supposed to be attracted to creatures that were infinitely larger than him. Massive females that would coil with him when they wanted a child. Someday, he would do the same thing that his sister's mate had done. Although, he hoped he survived the mating, unlike his sister's chosen.

There was something rather magical about seeing a female that was smaller than him. First, he had thought it was a child. Surely something so small would not be full grown.

But then he'd realized there was no one else in the strange circular shell. It was just her, and another voice that seemed to come out of the walls of the strange contraption. Which meant she couldn't be a child. No one would send a child on a mission out into the ocean alone, not even her kind.

So he'd gone a little closer, wrapped his tail around it to keep the small shell in place while he watched her movements. She'd even spoken to him a few times, at least attempting to converse, and he didn't... well. He wasn't sure what to do with that.

Imber hadn't told any of his pod what he'd found. How could he? They would want to hunt her down, to see what this strange creature was who had captivated him. And though he was more than happy to help his pod in any way that he needed to, he didn't want to share this new secret just yet.

Which was why he had gone back to the kelp grove for multiple days in a row. And why he found himself in the same place, just like every other day. What if she came back? What if he got the chance to speak with her again?

He wasn't even sure what he would say. Should he tell her what he was? That he was one of the People of Water, and that there were many just like him? What if she wanted to discover his world?

Excitement zinged down his spine as he moved some of the kelp out of his way. The green bioluminescence of his body lit up like a beacon, casting a green glow upon the surrounding kelp. Somehow, he knew today was the day that he would see her again. There were too many good omens for her to not be here.

To his utter delight, the first thing he saw when he pushed aside the kelp was that strange shell that she rode in. It was lying against the sand again, although the dust had long since settled and there were more creatures swimming around it. Even the fish wanted to know what it was that had entered their home.

Gliding through the water, he approached the glass front. Peering into the shadows, he realized she wasn't inside of it. How? He had no idea. Surely it wasn't possible for her to leave the shell? Was it?

Arcing up over the top, he realized there was a way into the pod. Although it was currently filled with water and then sealed again, it appeared there was a way for her to exit without flooding the entire space. And a small tube came out of the top, trailing out with plenty of slack.

"A tube?" he muttered, picking it up in his hands and giving it a small squeeze. "Flexible, but... for what reason?"

Was this how she ate? Was the shell itself actually the creature she served, and she was just the bait to draw things back into the shell for food?

Horrified at the mere thought, he told himself to get control of himself. She was not some mythical creature who served a giant metal god. He had seen her kind many times before, and they were individual creatures that were intelligent enough to create something like this shell. Not the other way around.

Still, he hesitantly trailed the strange tube through the kelp forest. The last thing he needed was to die on the day his sister gave birth. They'd call his spirit to them just so they could yell at him for being such an idiot on a special day.

Frowning, he picked up the tube again in his hand and felt it loosely drawing through his fingers. Surely she was close... ah. There. He brushed the kelp aside to see her floating above a large rocky outcropping, staring down into the sheer drop off that continued on for hundreds and hundreds of meters. That was the very bottom of the ocean down that drop off, although he doubted she had any way of knowing that.

Carefully, so he didn't surprise her, he tugged on the tube. It was connected to something she wore around her face, and he had no idea how it was helping her. The achromos that he'd seen before couldn't breathe underwater.

Without looking behind her, she tugged back.

Again, he tugged. Insistent that she look at him so he didn't have to swim right up to her and scare her into the abyss. "Achromo," he said quietly, although he knew his voice could be booming in the water. "What are you doing?"

She let out a shriek that would rival the killer whales that ruled this area of the ocean. The sound made his ears hurt so badly that he lifted his hands to cover them, but that also meant he tugged harder on the tube. She shrieked again, this time dragged closer by his movements as she desperately hung onto the thing attached to her head.

Why did that matter?

She was screaming so loud he was going to lose his ability to hear, and all she could do was hang onto that stupid tube going to her...

Suddenly the achromo catapulted toward him. He hadn't

realized she could move quite so fast, or he would have put more distance between the two of them. He braced himself, flaring his fins wide to prepare for her attack. Imber was much larger than her, and he would hurt her if he had to. Didn't she see his claws? Hadn't she seen his fangs when he'd bared them in surprise after her shell suddenly came to life?

She hit him hard. Harder than he'd expected for someone so small. And in that moment, he realized two very startling things. First, she had two tails. Two bony, horrible feeling tails that wrapped around him like a crab grabbing onto its prey. The second was that she was so very soft.

He planted his hand against her back, his claws ready to rend her flesh from her bone and leave her bleeding out on the ground. But he hesitated when she did nothing other than cling to him, her form so warm against his usually cool skin. Those tails held him in place as she reached for his wrists.

He thought perhaps she wished to speak with him, but that wasn't what she was doing. Instead, she drew the tube out of his hand and let it drift in the water beside them.

She was so close. Closer than he'd ever anticipated getting to one of her kind. White surrounded the pale blue of her eyes. All those golden curls billowed around her head, creating a terrible tangle of curls and coils that would be nearly impossible to brush out. But his gaze caught on the soft swells of her cheeks, the paleness of her lips that he remembered being much darker. And the wide eyes that stared directly into his own, as though she were overwhelmed with what she saw.

Garbled sounds came out of her mouth, and though he had no idea what she was saying, he could guess.

"I'm sorry to have startled you." And because he couldn't not touch her—what man had such inner strength?—he lifted his hand to brush a strand of her hair aside. "I was trying not to."

She seemed to freeze in his arms as he touched her. Growing bolder now, he let the back of his nail drag down the plushness of her cheek. She shivered, and he couldn't tell if that was from fear or something else entirely.

Some small whisper in his mind hoped it was something else. He hoped she didn't see him as some monstrous creature who had risen out of the depths to tear her away from life itself. He wanted to... He wasn't sure what he wanted, really. Anything dancing through his mind right now must be an abomination and he should never be thinking it.

He just wanted. Her attention, her gaze, her.

Everything always seemed to boil down to this magical creature who shouldn't be here and yet, here she was.

"Where did you come from?" he whispered, trying to keep his voice as quiet as possible. "You seem to have appeared out of thin air, achromo."

Curious little thing. Though her strange tails still gripped him around the waist with surprising strength, she used her web free hands to touch him. First she hovered just over his forehead, watching his movements with wide eyes, as though she was afraid he would tell her no.

He didn't. How could he? The first moment those warm fingertips trailed twin lines down his forehead, to his temples, and then just barely over his gills, he knew he was a goner.

No one touched him so gently. Not even his mother. He was a creature made to hunt and kill, that was all. Their kind were brutal to live in the waters that tried to kill them. Gentleness wasn't in their nature.

Perhaps, if he was lucky, he would find himself a mate who knew how to control herself during a mating. She might not kill him, and then he could be gentle with his own child.

Imber had never hoped to feel a female touch him like this. He hadn't even known it existed.

Groaning, he tilted his head back and let her bury her fingers in his hair. She seemed particularly interested in the gills at his neck and also the texture of the long strands of his hair.

Surely she didn't know the intimacy with which she touched

him. How would she know that every stroke along his body was telling him that he should prepare himself for mating? That she wanted him. Needed him. Desired him.

Another low groan echoed through his entire chest, and he felt the gills along his ribs begin to flutter. The choked sound that came out of her at the movement was intriguing. Cracking open an eye, he drew in a deep breath of a scent that fascinated him. It was coming from her.

Maybe she really was touching him to prepare him to mate with her.

Suddenly, the pale one untangled herself from his body. She lunged away from him, moving those short, useless tails until there was space between them. Space for both of them to breathe, which he realized he desperately needed to do.

His scales had clasped onto her scent, he realized with horror. His body wanted to keep her on him so that all others would know that he was entertaining a female.

The pod would know.

His family would know that he'd seen a female and covered himself in her scent. What a fool he was! He couldn't afford this, not when he was already struggling to find a mate of his own. He didn't...

By all the gods of the sea, she was pretty.

With her hair all spiraled around her head like that, he could easily see how red her cheeks had become. She turned different shades of lovely mottled red, and he had never thought her kind could do that.

"If you're interested in me," he started, trying hard to clear his throat and not sound too eager, "We may perhaps speak of this, achromo. I do not know your kind, nor have I ever considered trying to see what is possible between our species. But I am willing to try if you are."

She had no way of understanding him, but he thought perhaps he had startled her. She said nothing in return, not that he could understand her either. But as she swam by him, making sure he didn't move as she passed by, she reached out and trailed her fingers along his shoulder. He reached for her, spinning only his torso as she let her fingers glide along the entire length of his arm.

And oh, her scent hadn't changed. That musky, delicious scent made his mouth water as she gathered up the tube in her arms and swam away from him. It was slow going, and she used her hands to pull herself faster.

A mate like her would be difficult to keep safe. She was so small, and clearly couldn't fight for herself. She wasn't cut out to live in the ocean either, although he knew that was a silly thing to even consider.

But as he swam behind her, keeping out of her line of sight so she thought she was fleeing from him, he could still smell her need. Her desire. And he knew without a doubt she would be back.

This time, he would be ready for her.

CHAPTER
Three

PERHAPS SHE'D LOST her mind. That was the only thought that brought Alys back to the same kelp forest every single week. Then it became twice a week. Multiple times a week. Almost every day.

Her father was going to realize soon that she wasn't researching the area. He was a shrewd man with an eye for her habits, and she knew that sooner or later she'd have to answer to him. But right now, she was enjoying herself far too much.

Stalling the submarine in the same spot where she had been leaving it for days on end, she waited while holding her breath. Her eyes locked on the kelp in front of her, every muscle in her body seized as she waited.

"This is getting ridiculous," her droid muttered inside the wall. "Eventually you're going to have to do something other than stare at him."

"I'm not staring at him," she replied. "I'm waiting for him."

"Sure looks like staring to me."

They couldn't even speak with each other, but that didn't matter to Alys. They talked in other ways. Hand gestures, heart felt looks. She knew without a doubt that he found her as interesting as she found him. And together, they were discovering so much about each other's species.

As far as she knew, no other human had seen a species like his. Sure, there were plenty of creatures in the ocean they knew very little about. Fish and crabs and wild looking octopi, those were all being discovered by countless droids that were assigned to certain scientists. But had anyone made contact with a species that had a language and emotions and... looked so eerily human when they felt strong emotions?

The kelp parted around a darkened hand, the flash of green scales already letting her know that he was here for her. The grin on her face almost hurt as she bolted toward the hatch above her.

Alys had made sure to wear something pretty today. Usually she wore clothing that was practical for swimming. She chose tight-fitting pants and wetsuits that allowed her to at the very least be warm. But the water here was already warmer.

The volcanoes had finally stopped their madness, which meant she could easily swim in this water because everything was still pretty warm. At least she wasn't boiling or freezing. She'd take it.

So today, she'd worn a dress. A bright blue dress with a tight bodice and many layers of skirts that she knew would billow around her prettily in the water. She wanted to see what he thought about a dress. She wanted to feel... pretty to him.

Because he was so thoroughly intriguing to her.

Placing her goggles and air over her mouth, she made sure the door beneath her was sealed into the more electronic parts of the sub and then opened the final hatch. The water rushed in so quickly she had to brace herself against the wall with all her limbs.

But this time, a strong arm reached in with it and drew her out with ease. When he did things like that, it always made her breathless.

He was so strong. Alys didn't need to see him draw her out of the submarine, as though the suction in that room wasn't enough to send her careening back into the sub. She could see it in the rippling muscles of his shoulders and the way his chest flexed. She could see it in the anchoring of his tail around her ship and how easily he tugged her against his heart.

He was...

She didn't have words for it. She wished she did.

Alys shook her head. Her palms pressed against his cool chest when she realized for all the time that they had been together, they'd only been experiencing his world. He'd taken her swimming and taught her how to swim better and faster. He had brought her seashells and fish from the depths of the sea. They had laughed at each other's antics, but she'd never asked his name.

Reaching for his face, she trailed a single finger down his forehead, cheek, to his jaw. She was so comfortable touching him, when she'd never been comfortable touching anyone else like this. Not a human, that was for certain.

"What is your name?" she asked, her voice little more than a breathless whisper.

He arched a dark brow, that devastatingly handsome face wrinkling with confusion.

Swallowing, she touched a finger to her forehead. "Alys." Then she tapped his forehead.

He didn't seem to understand what she was asking, so she did it a few more times. Never saying anything other than her name. Then suddenly she could see the realization dawn on him. His eyes widened, his lips parted in sudden shock.

"Alys," he repeated, that low voice singing the word. She'd never heard the sound of her own name be so beautiful.

Reaching up between them, he traced her jaw with a long claw. "Alys," he said again, then rumbled a word that she would never forget. "Imber."

"Is that your name?" she breathed. "Imber?"

His entire face brightened with the word as she said it, and she knew she was right. His name was Imber, and it was such a strange name for a man so large and dangerous.

Yet, he was still holding onto her. Sinking away from the sub and allowing the current to gently nudge them toward the kelp. He relaxed, allowing his body to almost lay flat in the water as she sat draped on top of him.

Naturally, her legs fell to either side of his body. Naturally, she wanted him.

Maybe it made her some kind of deviant. She didn't know anyone else who would see a monster from the depths and find him attractive, but she was lost in him. In the hard angles of his features, the blackness of his eyes, and the green scales that abraded her palms as she slid them down his chest, ribs, and sides.

Everywhere she touched him felt like molten metal. Or maybe it just made her hot to touch him. There was definitely something wrong with her.

And yet, sometimes she looked at his eyes and saw an answering flash of interest. As though he knew what was going through her mind every time she dragged her fingers down his sides. Every time she had the opportunity to drape herself over his chest just like this.

He knew. He had to know.

Somehow, she wasn't embarrassed by that knowledge, either. She was so happy that he was with her, and that made all the difference.

Sighing, she rested her head as comfortably as she could against his chest. The tube got in the way, and the mouthpiece wasn't all that comfortable to wear when she was touching something else. But it felt right to lie against him and just... be.

"Did you bring me anything to see today?" she asked, drawing a pattern on his pectorals as they finally reached the kelp forest. "You usually bring me some interesting things from the depths."

As if he understood what she was asking, he reached underneath them to draw out a small bag he must have left in the kelp forest. He popped it onto his chest, as if he also knew that she didn't want to move from where she was. At least, not yet.

She straddled him, sitting up on his abs so she could rip into the bag without ever having to stop touching him.

Healthy? No. This entire relationship would likely end in one of them dying. She'd either drown, or he would accidentally kill her. That's what her father would say, at the very least. But for now, she wasn't going to think about the fact that she was straddling a very dangerous creature, or that he was rubbing his hands up and down her thighs as she pulled the bag open.

Inside was the most beautiful shell she'd ever seen. Abalone, she thought it was called, but it was every color of the rainbow. It had been meticulously carved into the image of what looked like a wave. A swell that crested into the white exterior of the shell and then dove into swirling patterns of water.

"It's beautiful," she whispered, although her attention was certainly pulled away from it when his hands squeezed the meat of her thighs. He shouldn't do that. He shouldn't toy with fate.

They were two different species. And while he was clearly intelligent, a creature who was very much capable of learning and emotion and all the other things that made her human... How would they fit?

Alys knew without a doubt she flirted with going against nature as she looked down into his pleased gaze. But she supposed it didn't really matter in the end.

She was here. He was underneath her, and she had never been so thankful for anyone before. He looked at her like actually saw her. She wasn't the daughter of an inventor who had changed the lifespan of humans across the globe. She wasn't the girl who had to live up to her father's impressive deeds.

Imber looked at her and he saw Alys. The daredevil who perhaps took a few too many risks, but who wanted the world to see her as someone other than the girl who lived in her father's shadow.

He touched a finger to the carving and then tapped his claw to her forehead. As if trying to tell her something.

"This is for me?" she curled her hand around it and mimed like she was going to put it in her pocket.

A deep thrum started in his chest. He slid his hand with hers inside her pocket, the backs of his fingers brushing against her hip bone. But then he said something else, his eyes intense. Sliding his hand out of her pocket, he dragged his fingers through her skirts and then flattened his hand above her chest. Above her heart.

As if...

"Is the carving supposed to be me?" she asked. Tapping her hands against her chest, she said, "Alys?"

He touched the carving in her pocket and gently patted his hand over her heart at the same time. "Alys." Then he said another word. Maybe two, she didn't know.

All she understood was that he saw her like he saw the sea itself.

A thud made her chest hurt. Then another. Then she realized that something inside of her was screaming to get out, because he saw her like the sea. He saw her as some goddess who had walked into his life, a wave that crashed down upon him and he wasn't afraid of that.

Imber did not fear the wildness in her or the risks she took. He saw her as the mad woman who so many people disliked in her community because of her adventurous personality, and he enjoyed it.

This undine had carved her a message. Her wildness did not scare him, and he admired her for it.

Something snapped inside her. She ripped the mouthpiece off her face and kissed him. She didn't care that she couldn't breathe, or that she might not be able to reattach the mouth piece in time. Right now, the risk was worth kissing him.

He stilled at her movement, seemingly surprised at what she was doing. And maybe his people didn't kiss, but the moment she moved her mouth against his, her tongue sliding against his lips, he seemed to get it.

A low growl rumbled through his chest. Those gills on his ribs rippled against her inner thighs, and then his arms snapped around her. He dragged her tightly against him, almost crushing her against his chest as his lips parted and he devoured her.

Teeth and tongue, licking and biting as he learned the taste of her. The sensation of her mouth against his. Who needed air when she could simply breathe him in?

Eventually, the need to breathe made her entire body spasm. She wanted air, but she also wanted to keep kissing him, and what a cruel world it was that she couldn't. She wanted to touch him, hold him, make him more hers with every moment.

His claws dug into her thighs, and she could feel the indentations of his hands against her skin. She knew she would have marks there later. That when she was alone later tonight, she would pull her skirts up to see the tiny pinpricks of blood, and it would make her even more excited than she was now. She would...

Again her body spasmed, this time her heart thudding awkwardly in addition as it warned her there were only so many more seconds before she would breathe in water and start to drown.

But then he reached up between them. His hand glided along her side, his fingers skimming over her breast and up her throat. She arched into him, even if it meant that she was taking precious moments away from when she should be slamming that mouth piece over her mouth.

He... pinched her nose?

And then he exhaled.

Oh.

Her lungs filled with air that he breathed into her mouth, and she greedily sucked it down. Every exhale he gave her was a few more moments when she could keep tasting him. Moments when she could dig her own hands into the muscles of his shoulders, leaving the little half moons against his skin as she begged him to keep breathing. To prolong this moment.

She didn't know how long they kissed. She had no way of knowing the passage of time, only that eventually she had to stop making out with him like a teenager because another loud booming noise echoed through the ocean.

It sounded fairly similar to how he spoke, although it was not a word she was used to hearing. Or perhaps it was another language, but one he understood.

He stiffened underneath her and pulled their lips away. Without even looking at her, he placed her mouthpiece over her face.

Apparently, everything was done. Considering how tense he was underneath her thighs, she had a feeling that was for good reason. Already he'd flicked his tail, moving, so she was clinging to him rather than lying on top of him. They were moving back toward the sub. She struggled to fit the mouth piece over her face correctly, and there was some water in it around her chin, but she exhaled the last of the air out of her lungs and gave herself a small bubble from which she could breathe.

"What is it?" she asked, her eyes wide as he handed her up to the top of the sub where she usually entered.

His hands flexed around her waist, and she let herself believe he didn't want to let her go. Even his gaze said that as he looked at her, those dark eyes conveying so much that she hoped she was reading correctly.

But then he moved to put her inside the sub, and she knew her time was up.

"I'm going," she mumbled, then reached out to trail her fingers over his lips. "This was..."

He said something, and whatever it was, she took it to heart. That he didn't want her to go. That this was a life-changing experience for both of them and he was thanking her for every-thing that had happened.

Or something along those lines.

He flicked his tail, disappearing into the kelp, and left her to get back inside the sub. She buckled herself in, soaking wet and likely ruining some of the functions. Of course, Beta had a lot to say about that, but she didn't listen to the little droid.

Alys was in her own world. Even as she docked the sub above ground at the port where she and her father kept their submarines and ships. She didn't even notice that she'd walked through the hall to the kitchen, leaving wet footprints in her wake.

She didn't notice that her father was sitting at the kitchen island, waiting for her, until she heard his guttural tones.

"Where have you been, Alys?"

CHAPTER
Four

JUST BECAUSE SHE hadn't been here for a few days didn't mean she no longer wished to see him.

At least, that's what he told himself every day he showed up in their grove and she wasn't there.

He wasn't a fool. Imber knew whatever was between them was risky. Alys was one of the achromos, and he was one of the People of Water. He didn't even know how they would make this relationship work. She couldn't breathe underwater. He couldn't live on the land. They were the sun and the sea, trying very hard to make something work between the two of them, but knowing that eventually, they had to part.

The moon always rose on the horizon, and the sun always set. No matter how hard the waves tried to chase the sun.

Was it so terrible that he wished to try? He would chase her throughout all the nights of his life. Waiting for the briefest hint of her sunshine, because she made him feel so much better than he did in the pod.

Even the day when his sister, Virago, found him, he had thought to show Alys to his sister. Perhaps his sister would understand his feelings, because she had gone for a much smaller male than the others who had fought for her attention.

She wasn't like the other people in their pod. Surely she would realize he'd made a connection with someone without knowing how to stop himself.

But he hadn't been able to put her at risk. His Alys was so tiny, so gentle. Virago would take one look at her and tell him that she wasn't worth being a partner to anyone. Alys wouldn't make strong children, nor could she protect them.

And yet, he still wanted to be the one to help her through it. He still wanted to be the one who defied the odds and protected his children for the both of them. He wanted... her.

A future with her. A life that was filled with the sound of her giggles and the soft touch of her hair stroking against his chest.

He wanted to feel her in his life. To know that every time he returned home, she was waiting for him there. It was an impossible future and yet, he would do anything to have it.

He gathered up his newest gift to give her. He'd been working on finding pearls inside of clams that they usually used for feasts. The clams were all too happy to get the granule of sand out of their shells, and he knew the tricks to getting them out without killing the animal. At least, until they needed them for a feast.

As it was, he had a handful of pearls that he'd woven with the strands they gathered from the thin ocean weeds. But he feared that it wouldn't last long out of the sea. He'd never tried to see what happened to the seagrass when it was dried out. They had no reason to keep anything dry underwater.

But his Alys always seemed to arrive to him dry, and then quickly jumped into the water. He'd noticed that she started coating her hair with something every time she got into the water. It meant her curls that he was so fascinated with were rarely on display anymore.

How frustrating it was that he couldn't talk to her and ask about all the things that piqued his curiosity.

"Brother." The voice made him pause on the edge of their pod home. They were a shallow water tribe, unlike many of his people who lived in the deep depths of the sea. As such, most of their homes were very easy to see into. They all gathered stones and made swirling patterns dug into the sand, like fish nests. Yet sometimes they had coverings over the top, for a sense of privacy.

He, unfortunately, did not have such a barrier.

Glancing up toward the surface, he saw his sister hovering above him. She looked so much like him, although nearly twice as large. Strong shoulders, strong arms, her hair cropped close to her skull. But their scales were the same color, the same vibrant green that graced his belly, also speckled along hers. Even their fin shapes were the same, diamond and ragged as they aged and the thin membranes slowly ripped. Her belly was still slightly bloated after having the child weeks ago, and she kept her daughter wrapped up in thick kelp weeds so the child was tied to her hip at all times.

Otherwise, his little niece was apt to get in trouble. She'd already slipped away more times than any of them could count. Even now, the little one was wriggling her tail, trying to get out of the slippery kelp so she could launch herself into Imber's arms.

He tried very hard not to smile and nodded at the child. "You're going to lose her again."

"Oh for..." His sister muttered curses underneath her breath, mostly all aimed at the child's father before scooping her up in her arms and holding onto the child firmly. "I'm going to start tethering her tail to me. You know she inherited this behavior from her father."

"Most likely."

"She needs to calm down. Maybe once we name her, she'll be able to fit better into the life she's supposed to live." Virago lifted her child up to her face, frowning at the giggling baby. "Enough, for once. I need to speak with your uncle."

The baby gurgled a bit, but eventually quieted down.

Virago sighed, as though soaking in the silence for a few

moments before she tied her daughter back to her hip. "Where have you been disappearing to everyday?"

"I've been seeking out new hunting grounds."

"Yes, there are many who might believe that, but not me, brother." The glare on her face told him that she didn't even remotely trust that he was telling the truth. "If you're going to tell anyone, you might as well tell me."

He sighed, raking his claws through his hair. "I have met... someone."

"Someone?"

"She is kind and different, Virago. I do not know where it is going at the moment, so I'm just allowing it to play out as it will." The lie tasted acidic on his tongue.

He knew where he wanted it to go, at the very least. And he knew that the two of them had a connection he'd never seen before with his pod. They were bound, he and Alys, but he didn't know where that was going to put the two of them.

They had a long way to go before either of them figured that out.

Virago's eyes trailed along his face, as though she knew what he was struggling with. As though she could read his mind.

"You are being careful?" she asked.

"I am."

"Then you should be more careful than you are now." Her eyes narrowed even further. "I know you, brother. I can smell her on your scales when you swim by. You are coating yourself in her scent, and I'm not sure you know what that means."

"I know what it means." Imber tried very hard not to bristle at her tone. "I am not a child."

"No, you are my older brother and yet I am the one always reminding you to not take risks." She held out her hand for him, drawing him out of his stone nest and up into the ocean with her. Her child grabbed onto one of his hip fins, giving it a rather painful tug.

"Your words come from a place of caring, I know that."

Imber took his time gently unwinding her child's fingers from his hip fins. "She is different, sister."

"Then why have we not met her yet?"

Because she was an achromo. Because she had two tails, and he still hadn't figured out how they worked yet. Because Alys was nothing like his family, and he feared they would take one look at her and see her as nothing more than a liability.

He swallowed all those words down and instead replied with, "I'm not ready to introduce her to you. But when I am, I will make sure you are the first to meet her."

Virago reached for the back of his neck, drawing his forehead to hers and sighing. He could feel the current created by the deep breath through her gills, and he was reminded that this was his sister. She loved him, even if she was a little rough around the edges.

Gripping her forearms, he gave her a little squeeze before moving back. "Keep watch over that child of yours. I don't want to find her at the drop off again."

Virago rolled her eyes. "It was one time, brother! One time. She hasn't gone back to the drop off in ages."

"Days," he scolded. "Days, Virago."

"A long time in the mind of a child. She's long forgotten it even exists."

He rolled his eyes and sped away, listening to the sound of his sister's laughter. That child was a wild thing, but he supposed she had gotten that from her mother.

Speeding through the waves, he made his way to their meeting spot with his heart in his throat. He hoped she was there this time. He knew that hope was dangerous, though. Especially after all the disappointment that he'd suffered through the past week. She had no reason to visit him often. Neither of them had made any promises, but he had hoped they had developed something that she could see. Especially after that kiss.

Oh, that kiss had haunted his dreams every night.

Maybe she'd gotten tired of him. But his twin beating hearts raced with the truth that she would never get tired of him. Not that easily.

Something must have happened, and today was the day he would see her again. He was certain of it.

Imber was breathing hard by the time he made it to the kelp grove, but all that breath left his lungs when he saw her sub. It wasn't settled on the sand as sturdily as normal, either. Little electric waves of nerves burst through his body, lighting up his fins bright green as he noticed that it was almost on its side. Like she'd landed in a hurry.

He frowned, his gaze sweeping to see where she was and if she had been followed. Why else would she have landed like something was wrong? Someone must have tracked her here. Perhaps she was in trouble.

The spines along his back rose, and he could feel his body starting to loosen. Already he could make the slick oil that would cover his skin, giving him even more speed in the water should he need it. Though he was not as large as his sister, he was still a fighter. All of his people were fighters. He could kill anyone who had tracked her to this place, and he would keep her safe.

But her tube of air was out of the shell that she traveled in, so surely she was around here somewhere.

It took a few moments of tracking for him to pick up the air tube and follow her as long as it could go. And there she was. Not smelling of blood or anything else dangerous. She sat on the very edge of the ledge that disappeared into blackness, staring down into the darkness like she was thinking about swimming down and exploring it.

Unlike the first time he'd found her here, he wasn't so concerned about startling her. Instead, he curved wide around the ledge, diving into the darkness before she could see him.

Then he let all the lights on his body flicker to life. Bright green and emerald, he floated out of the darkness and drifted toward her. He could see her so clearly. The way her eyes widened in surprise and the delighted smile that spread across her face.

He'd done that. Just by showing up in front of her.

"Imber," she said, his name a breathy whisper as he approached her.

He'd do anything to hear her say his name a hundred times over. And maybe that was moving too fast. Maybe he was immature because he was so obsessed with her.

A part of him feared that all of his interest was wrapped up in her merely because he'd never seen anything like her before in his life. Every day, he worried that the newness of her would wear off. That he would wake and be less interested than he was the day before.

Maybe that day would come. Or maybe his twin hearts in his chest knew something that he did not.

He reached for her, his hands brushing aside the billowing layers of her skirt and drawing her against his chest. She wrapped herself around him so easily, twining her twin tails around his waist and tucking her face into the hollow of his neck. He breathed her into his gills, letting her scent ease the nerves that had plagued him since he'd had to say goodbye the last time.

Running his hands up and down her body, he soothed his worries by feeling that she was all in one piece. She wasn't injured, and that was good. He could hold on to that.

But she drew back all too soon. Babbling in that language that he couldn't quite make out. She spoke in such short, clipped words. Like the dull echo of stones clicking against each other, buried beneath the weight of the sea.

Then she thrust something into his hands. A small box made out of the same hard shell as her ship. Frowning, he lifted it up, trying to see what it could be.

"I have a gift for you as well." He hoped she liked the necklace he had woven. He hoped it wasn't too big, in fear she might lose it on her ride home.

She was backing away, though. Before he could reach into his bag. Before he could take anything out, she was already moving away from him. Shaking her head as though she didn't want to listen to him speak.

He held out his hand, frowning, hoping she would reach forward and slip her fingers into his. "Alys."

Something sparkled in her eyes, and it made him sad to see the expression before she spun and used the rocks below to yank herself away from him.

The box in his hand hummed. "Gift. Speak."

"I don't think we'll ever be able to learn each other's language," he muttered before realizing *the box had talked.*

Horrified, he dropped it.

As it careened down toward the darkness, he had two lightning quick thoughts. First, she'd given him some kind of abomination that could speak. And second, that it was the only gift she'd ever given him and he would be an idiot if he lost it.

Darting after the box, he got lucky when it hit a rocky outcropping before it would have plummeted far beyond his reach. Catching it in his hands, he leaned against the stone wall for a few moments, breathing hard and squeezing his eyes shut.

"I have you," he said, his voice ragged. "I have you."

"Gift. Special. Gift. Language."

He had no idea what it was trying to say.

It was a special gift because she had given it to him, yes. Perhaps she thought they could speak through it, but it clearly knew very little of his language. Lifting it up a little higher, he tried to peer into the faint blue light that emanated from a thin line around the top. "You do not know as much of my language as you think, little friend."

"Language. Learn."

"You..." It all hit him at once. "Did she give you to me to learn your language?"

"Yes."

She was... she was trying to learn how to speak with him. Not a gift, but a tool.

His hearts thundered again, beating against his ribs at the mere thought of speaking with her. He could talk to Alys. Actually talk to her. Listen to what she had done and where she had come from. He could tell her about his own adventures and see her eyes shine with happiness when he told her stories that were so detailed, she would never question the truthfulness of where they came from.

"How?" he asked. "How do you learn my language?"

The blue light glowed a little brighter. "Speak."

"All I have to do is speak to you?"

Another pulse of blue illuminated the water around them. "Speak," it repeated.

If that's all it took, then she had given the right person this box. He would speak until his throat went raw and his gills bled, if it meant he could converse with her.

CHAPTER

Five

THE FIRST CONVERSATION with her father about where she had been didn't go so well. Alys had sat for a very long time, waiting for him to calm down. He had yelled, screamed, even threatened to take away her submarine because she refused to tell him where she had been going.

But she knew better. She would not tell him the secret she had with Imber. Her father wouldn't understand the man who had found her in the sea. Nor would he care that they had a connection.

All he would see was that there was another person in the ocean. Another creature that would threaten his ability to build wherever he wanted. And though she loved his ability to see the future in a different way... she didn't want to waste what she had, either.

Imber was a secret she would keep. If that meant she had to stay away from him for weeks on end because her father would surely follow her, then so be it.

She hated staying away from him, though. Life above the sea had already lost its luster long before she met the undine. She was the strange girl. The daughter who had so much responsi-bility and expectation on her shoulders. And even though she loved her father, more than he would ever know, she also was very aware of his flaws.

Especially lately. She didn't know how to tell him that she was frightened for him. He'd gotten so lost in his work. Like he could see a future that no one else could, but also that he was fighting for something that might never exist.

He didn't sleep. He barely ate. He just focused on the project of creating Alpha. The city that would sink beneath the sea and keep all of humanity safe for ages to come.

But that wasn't entirely right, now was it? Alpha was going to be a beautiful city and humans would live in it for years on end. It was still a city under the sea. It wasn't life up here. Living as humans were meant to do, in the air with the land underneath their feet.

Finally, she couldn't take it anymore. She packed up her things, making sure there was enough air supply in her ship to get her to the places she needed to go, and enough fuel to get her there and back. She packed an extra set of clothing so no one would be able to ask where she had gone.

And then she wrote a letter, leaving it on her desk in case her father got curious about where his wayward daughter had gone off to. She was not going to get in trouble this time.

"Don't feel too guilty about lying," she told herself. "Your father wouldn't let you go, and really, you are stopping by the dig site along the way, aren't you?"

Sneaking through the halls, she found herself lingering outside her father's office.

Alys did that sometimes. She just... stood there. Waiting. Maybe she liked hearing her father's voice. Or maybe it was just knowing that he was there, on the other side of the door.

But this time, there was another voice as well.

"Listen to me, Fairweather." The deep voice was almost familiar, although she couldn't place where she had heard it before. "The city will be built whether we destroy the ecosystem or not. You said it yourself. It will be easier to build if it's on flat land."

Her father cleared his throat, and she could sense how uncomfortable he was with the conversation. "Yes, but there is the conversation with the architects we need to uphold. Aesthetic is considered to be one of the greatest things we can do for this build. And aesthetic means that we build it around what is currently there. Alpha is meant to be functional *and* beautiful. It is a showcase of what the human mind can conjure."

"And it will be the most heavily fortified city underneath the sea. How are we meant to fortify it without having a clear view of everything around us?"

She knew who spoke this time.

The General.

He had come from a long line of men who had essentially taken control over what was left of humanity. No more presidents or kings or rulers. Just a general with the entire army at his beck and call. There was nothing for them to fight against, so why they needed a general she had never understood. Maybe it was because he could kill anyone who disagreed with him.

Alys hadn't realized her father was working with this man.

"I understand your primary concern is safety," her father started, clearly trying to choose his words wisely. "But we need to build a place that is both safe and feels like home. Otherwise, no one will move there."

"I think you're underestimating the circumstances. We only have a few more years on land. At best. The volcanoes are erupting more frequently. The storms are getting worse. Soon, all life will be wiped out. If we have nowhere else to go, then those who wish to survive will join us."

"A few years?" her father choked. "I need far more than that to design a functional city under the sea! This will take a lifetime of work, perhaps even a lifetime more of architects to design something that is safe."

"You don't have years, Fairweather. And you have a working

design currently. Don't think I don't see it. You are afraid that your design isn't what you think it is, and so you are stalling. I understand fear. I know what you fight against, but the beast must die. Give me the design, and I will have it built in a year."

"It's simply not possible. You will destroy too much in doing so."

"I will destroy whatever I must."

Heart in her throat, Alys slipped out of the house. She didn't know where she was running off to. Maybe to him. Probably to him, if she was being honest with herself.

And that was silly. She shouldn't go to the people whose homes her people were likely going to destroy. She shouldn't feel so guilty about this, either. Her people had to survive, and they didn't realize that the undines were there. Right?

Surely they didn't.

But that pit in her stomach did not loosen. No matter how much distance she put between herself and those men, she couldn't stop thinking about what they were going to do.

Imber deserved to know. But she didn't have any way to communicate this with him, and what if he didn't understand what she wanted him to do? What if he realized that this would destroy his people, or could, and then there was a war that she started?

Panic had long set it by the time she got to their meeting spot. She didn't even know if he would be there waiting for her. So far, he usually was, but what if she was wrong?

The "what-ifs" turned her inside out. They ripped through her lungs, rioted in her stomach until she thought she might throw up.

"Miss Alys, your heart rate is dangerously high," Beta said, its voice echoing through the room. "You need to calm down before you go outside. I cannot promise there is enough oxygen in that tube to sustain your current body needs."

Hyperventilating. Her mind knew what was happening, and yet she was already ripping at the hatch over her head. She didn't care. She had to get out of this little bubble that her father had made because his touch was all over it.

What was he going to do? Was he really going to go along with this and ruin so much of the sea for... what? Glory? Honor? A legacy that would be forgotten about the moment he died?

"Miss Alys—"

She wasn't listening. She couldn't. Yanking the mouthpiece over her face, she slammed the button to close the door. Sealing Beta inside the sub even as she risked opening the top hatch, maybe a hair too soon. She was thrown against the wall of the submarine, her back catching on a piece of metal and searing pain slicing through her spine.

Still, she crawled her way out and blasted into the sea. She swam far above the sub and just let the sea buoy her. She could feel it moving all over her body. The currents gently held onto her, like the warm pressure of a hug. And the sun above her head glittered on a rare day when the sky wasn't full of ash.

She couldn't breathe. There wasn't enough air in the damn tube and her father was going to do something stupid. She couldn't tell the undines about this, not yet. All of this reaction was maybe just dramatics, and she didn't actually have to do any of this. Maybe her father would stop it. She had to believe in him.

Cool arms slid around her from behind.

Immediately, all the panic disappeared. It bubbled out of her mouth and suddenly she could breathe again. She could inhale, long and slow. Breathing in through her nose and out through her mouth as he drew her against his chest and held her safely in the circle of his arms.

"You came," she whispered, allowing her body to sag against his.

She let her eyes drift closed, allowing him and the current to rock her gently from side to side. Together they hung there, suspended where gravity had no rule on her body. Every now and then, she felt his tail shift between her legs, flicking to keep them afloat.

Finally, she was calm enough to open her eyes and practically liquid in his arms. Like he sensed it, he held something out in front of her.

The box. The copy of Beta that she'd given him. If he was giving it to her then... that had to mean... He touched something to the side of her head, and she knew it was a translation chip. Just like she had told Beta to make before, this box was no longer useful. It would then destroy itself once it had made two translation chips. One for him and one for her.

In awe, she took the box from him as his arm tightened slightly around her waist. He leaned down and murmured in her ear, "Hello, Alys."

Tears pricked in her eyes.

She could understand him! And those were the first words she heard, just like she would have if they were two people meeting on land. Like they didn't already have a massive amount of history between the two of them.

Slowly turning in his arms, knowing her eyes were wider than they had ever been before, she licked her lips and watched his mouth. "Say something else."

"You understand me?"

Words eluded her. Instead, she just nodded, her gaze still on his mouth.

"I don't know what to say now," he said with a slight chuckle. "Your strange creature gave me a small piece of metal to affix on the side of my head. It was not a comfortable experience."

"I didn't even notice it hurting." Probably because she had been shocked to hear his voice.

And oh, what a voice it was.

Everything in her suddenly fired, hot and wild. The depth of his voice was like watching molten caramel pour. It was deep and luxurious, flowing over her senses with specific words chosen slowly and with intent. She could listen to that melodic voice speak for hours on end. He could read her the dictionary and she would still be thinking how wonderful it was that he was speaking to her.

Looping her arms around his neck, she drew slightly closer to watch him speak. "Again."

"You have heard me speak before," he replied with amusement. Then suddenly they were moving. Drifting away from the submarine and through the kelp that brushed against her sides. Then his fingers brushed against her sides as well.

He stroked her body like he'd never touched her before. His fingers questing as he relearned the shape of her, draping her across him as he preferred while they floated and meandered through his world.

But now, they could speak. Suddenly, all of this felt very different. She could feel the heat of a blush burning her cheeks, and lying her head against his chest felt like maybe she was doing something wrong.

Shouldn't they... talk? Shouldn't they be learning about each other?

"I can feel you thinking," he said, his voice a low chuckle filled with humor. "You can speak about these worries now."

"I don't really know you," she whispered. "And you don't know me. What if this changes everything all of a sudden?"

"You think you don't know me?" Imber let them float down onto the soft gold sand. He sat up, his tail bracing her spine as he held her trapped against him. "After all the time we have spent together, you truly believe that I do not know your soul as well as my own?"

"Pretty words. But what if we have conjured up an image of the other person, not that we actually know each other?" That anxiety started creeping in again. Maybe she should tell him what she'd overheard.

Maybe she should let him know what her people were building underneath the sea, and how it would affect him directly. He needed to know the truth, because her people could be starting a war between all of them and he wouldn't be able to stop it.

Long claws dug into the back of her hair, drawing her close to him until their foreheads touched. "Breathe, my wave song. And listen to my words. Yes?"

She nodded against him.

"Our souls were called to each other long before you even saw me. You came to this place because the sea drew you here, knowing that the two of us needed each other. You are here after fate guided your hand. You understand that?"

"I don't believe in gods or fate."

"I believe in both enough for the two of us." And then this strange creature kissed her forehead, his lips lingering against her skin that was so much warmer than his. "This place, when we are together, it is a haven from the rest of the world. There are no responsibilities, no expectations. It is just you and I, wave song. The world doesn't exist here."

All the anxiety fled from her body yet again. Because he was right. The world didn't exist here.

It was just the two of them, and that made her happier than anything else. She was tainting this hidden place they had created between the two of them. If she wanted to let go of her stress, then all she had to do was let go of it.

Sighing, she eventually nodded and repeated, "The world doesn't exist here."

"No, it does not."

His hands moved from her hand, and then something heavy fell around her neck. Surprised, she looked down to see a string of lovely pearls woven together with emerald grass. She was almost scared to touch it, only feathering her fingers over it lightly. "What is this?"

"A gift."

"You always bring me gifts," she whispered, before looking

up at him with wide eyes. "I never bring you anything in return."

He shrugged and didn't seem bothered in the slightest. "I think of you often. So I bring you whatever makes me think of you."

"Pearls make you think of me?" She had never heard something so kind in her life.

Imber traced her fingers with his own, gently touching the delicate pearls and her collarbone in the same stroke. "They look the same as your skin. Pale, but with a hundred colors hidden underneath."

"I don't have any colors other than my skin," Alys snorted.

"Oh, you do." He moved his fingers, stroking her collarbone with intention this time. "You turn red here when I do something you like. And if I follow the line of your shoulder, there is the faintest hint of blue and purple where your veins are close to the skin. I've seen patches of yellow and green, where I think perhaps you have hurt yourself."

With her breath caught in her lungs, she didn't move at all when he moved her mouth piece up enough for his thumb to trace over her lower lip, gently pulling it down before he gave her back her air. "And you are so pink here. Especially after you've touched me with your mouth."

"A kiss," she replied. "That's what we call it."

His eyes somehow went from black to obsidian. "A kiss. I would like to kiss you again, Alys."

She groaned and let the world fall away. Who needed to breathe when he could breathe for her? Pouring desire and oxygen deep into her lungs with every broad stroke of his tongue.

CHAPTER
Six

SOMETHING WAS WRONG WITH ALYS.

Imber could tell that easily enough, even if she refused to tell him what was wrong. He'd asked, and even just in asking felt as though something had changed. She obviously knew he could sense when her emotions were off. Although, he didn't have the heart to tell her it was because he could taste them in the water.

He'd never met a creature easier to read. She wore her emotions like a second skin. Her desire was warm and musky, a scent that he regularly kept hidden under his scales for later, when he was alone. Her anxiety was bitter and noxious. It made him flatten his gills against his sides because it was hard to breathe in.

But lately, he had started to taste her fear. Bitter, acrid, it wriggled through every ounce of him and made his hearts beat faster with hers. When he'd asked her why she wasn't feeling well, she'd brushed him off. But he could tell something was wrong.

And he wasn't certain what it was, but he had a feeling it had something to do with her people.

Every time she went home, he had to fix her. She came to him to forget who she was, and she was getting thinner every time he saw her. Like she wasn't eating. Hollows had bruised underneath her eyes, which she said was because she hadn't been sleeping very well.

Just a week ago, she'd fallen asleep on top of him. Imber had cradled her against his chest, but he knew it wasn't enough to take her pain away. He'd have done anything to help her. She knew it. He knew it. But there was nothing she would tell him to do.

At a loss for what he could do for his beautiful wave song, he'd swallowed down his emotions. But now, watching her submarine leave him behind in the kelp, he couldn't stop the feeling that maybe he should follow her.

It was a silly thought. Even when he was a child, he had sought out the achromos. They were strange creatures, so different from his own, and many of his kind took the risk to see where they lived.

Even if he followed her home, he couldn't leave the water. And she would.

She always did.

Sighing, he tried to will his own nerves out of his body and into the waters. Let the ocean take his fears, because the ancients knew all. They would protect the People of Water.

But he feared...

Well, maybe he was just absorbing Alys's fears. He could let it go, even if it wanted to lodge itself in his throat.

The kelp beside him shifted, moving with a current that was rather unnatural to see. He assumed at first that it was a sea turtle, or perhaps a curious seal that had drifted a little farther than their normal hunting grounds. But then he caught a glimpse of bright green scales and he knew who it was.

For all that his sister was larger, and arguably should have been a better hunter than him, she had never been very good at hiding. Especially with a little one attached to her hip.

Leaning down to the sand, he scooped up a handful of the golden granules and let them trail between his fingers. "What do you think, Imber?" he said to himself, loud enough that his sister and her offspring would hear him. "Should we go hunting for oysters? Perhaps Virago's child would like to go pearl hunting."

The little one was born just as all of his people were. She could understand him easily. The long and low language with which they spoke had already been instilled in her long before she was born.

And he knew something his sister could never battle. The little one was a fiend for oysters. She loved slurping them down while finding the prettiest pearls with her uncle. No matter how hard Virago tried to keep her in the net that wrapped up her daughter, the little one would fight free with her sharp teeth and newly pointed spines to get to an oyster.

He heard the sound of struggling long before his sister's curse filled the air. Then a little arrow darted through the water toward him, her eyes wide and her hands already outstretched for whatever he held in his hand. Like he'd somehow plucked an oyster off the ground and prepared it just for her.

Now was the tricky part. If his niece realized he didn't have an oyster in his hand, she would dart off in another direction. The little one had a nose like a shark, and she would head to the nearest oysters in the vicinity. Of course, that would be a problem to find her. She was voracious, and would likely rip through the entire oyster strand before he or Virago had time to get to her.

Looping his tail, he gently flicked his fluke at the same moment she barreled toward him. The lightning quick child was immediately caught up in his much larger fluke that shoved her right into his waiting arms.

Catching her, he held onto her by the waist so she couldn't wiggle free. Her spines jabbed at the delicate webs between his fingers as she struggled.

Wincing, he held her wriggling body while her mother showed herself in the kelp.

"I thought we had said we weren't going to spy on each other," he grumbled, eyeing his sister. "That was a rule from when we were children. Need I remind you?"

"Yes, yes, well, we're all simply so curious about who you've been meeting that I had to be the one to see. Otherwise, it would have been one of the other younger ones." His sister shuddered. "The last thing you needed was someone else discovering you've been meeting with an achromo."

His entire world ground to a halt.

His sister knew.

Virago had seen him with Alys, which meant she knew he'd been meeting with someone who wasn't of their kind.

He had said for so long that he was meeting with a young woman that he was falling completely and utterly tail over head for. Everyone knew he wasn't even available anymore. They could smell Alys on him.

His pod was kind. They were more open than the other pods of their people, especially the ones that were deeper in the ocean. But he hadn't really given much thought to what they would do if he... if he...

Bringing her home to his people had never been an option, he realized. He risked losing everything if he did. And yet, if he lost Alys, then hadn't he already lost everything?

Breathing hard, he gulped and held his niece out from his body. Even though her tail slapped at his wrists, he couldn't stop staring at his sister in horror. "So what now?"

"What do you mean, what now?"

"What are you going to do?" Was she going to tell the pod? Would he have to leave everyone because he was the deviant who had covered himself in the scent of an achromo?

Virago looked at him with pity in her eyes. "Imber."

The single word wasn't enough of an answer. He needed to

know what she was going to do, because right now, she was the only one who could save him.

"Virago," he croaked. "None of it was a lie."

"None of it? You've been meeting with an achromo for weeks. Months, maybe. You've been telling stories about how you've found your mate, and how she makes you feel more complete than you ever hoped to feel." She grabbed her child, gently wrapping her back up in the net attached to her waist. "Was it because you didn't think you'd get to mate with anyone else? I know you're smaller than the other males, Imber. But clearly that doesn't matter. Look who I chose to mate with."

"And you killed him in the process," he muttered.

"A mistake." Virago at least looked a little guilty. "He was smaller than even I anticipated, but there are females smaller than me. A few scars later and you'd be a father. You're so good with your niece already, just think if she was your own."

He shook himself free from old thoughts. "I don't want a mate from our people, Virago. I've already found my mate."

His sister tilted her head back and laughed. Sharp teeth flashing, she looked somehow even more terrifying than usual with the mirth that made her shoulders wobble and the muscles on her belly visibly seizing before she got control of herself. "Hilarious, brother. But you don't have to lie to me."

He wasn't laughing with her. And it took a bit for her to realize that. "I'm not lying to you, Virago."

An awkward silence fell between them. Even the sea seemed to hold its breath, not moving a single current as the two siblings stared at each other. Imber refused to change what he had said, though. His sister needed to understand this wasn't some ruse, so the others would leave him alone.

Alys meant something to him. More than anyone else had ever meant, if he was being honest. She made his soul feel like he mattered. Like there was someone out there who saw him as more than just a potential mate. As more than someone who could bring life into this world.

"What?" Virago finally asked. "I don't understand what you're saying. You think that... that achromo is your mate?"

"I don't think she is my mate." He watched his sister deflate with relief, knowing that he was about to bring that tension back. "I know that she is. I choose her above all others, Virago. She is the one that the sea has sent for me."

"A soul bond?" his sister scoffed. "It is impossible with their kind. You have no idea what they are doing underneath the water. You haven't been going out on the scouting missions with the others. You haven't seen the madness they bring to our waters."

"I don't need to see anything to know how she makes me feel." He pressed a clawed hand to his chest, trying to convey how serious he was. "She sees me, sister. She makes me feel brave. When I speak, she laughs at what I say. She takes the gifts I give her and treats them like they are treasures that I stole from the gods themselves. And when she lies against my chest..." He tapped twice over each heart. "I feel that I am whole."

With every word, his sister's mouth dropped open wider and wider. If she wasn't careful, a fish was going to swim into that open maw of hers. And yet, she didn't close it even when he finished.

His statement hung between them. If he had been with any other person, he would have feared judgment. He would have worried they would slice him along the tail and leave him for the sharks after they decided he had clearly lost his mind.

But his sister wasn't like that. She understood that there were different people out there. She had chosen a male that no one else had ever thought she would choose because she saw the value in who he was.

Her mate had been a good man. And now his name was lost to the sea, because she had not been gentle enough to preserve him.

Virago snapped her jaws shut, the echoing click making him flinch. "You truly feel this way?"

"With both my hearts." He sighed. "I cannot explain the feeling much more than that, Virago. I know that I am where I should be when I am with her. And I know that she is not of our kind."

"You see how difficult it is going to be?"

"Of course I do." His words came out harsher than he'd intended, spitting them at his sister, who had always treated him like a child. "I see how difficult it is going to be. She cannot stay in the water forever, and I cannot go onto the land. But if I must chase her sunlight across the seas, I will. Just to bask in the light of her smile."

Something changed in Virago's expression. She went from confused and perhaps concerned, then calm and serene.

It was unnerving.

He flicked his tail to put distance between them. "What is that expression?"

It took her a while to respond, and when she did, he almost didn't hear the words. "I believe you, Imber."

He was... stunned. He hadn't thought she would believe him, let alone admit it. Imber had never dreamed it would be this easy for him to tell her, either.

This was his little secret. His greatest hope delivered to him in a package that his own people may very well never under-stand. How he wanted them to. He wanted them to see her and love her just as he did.

"Oh," he muttered, sinking down onto the sands with a horrified expression on his face. "Oh, no."

"What?" His sister's spines rose. She curved a clawed hand around her child, looking around for whatever danger might be upon them.

"I love her," he breathed. "I think I love her so very much. I might have loved her for a long time. But I just realized..."

Virago breathed out a sigh of relief, all the tension in her easing as she wrapped herself around him. Her tail flopped on top of his, heavy enough to squeeze out some of the anxiety. "Of course you do. You don't want her just as a mate, even I can see that. You want to keep her, Imber."

That was the problem, wasn't it? He couldn't keep her. No one could.

Trailing his hands over his niece's back, he let the soft skin remind him of what he had always wanted. A family. Someone to love him as much as he loved them. "I chose an impossible path, didn't I?"

"Maybe," Virago replied with a chuckle. "But you also could have chosen a path that changes the way we all see the world. Your achromo might be the reason we all need to help us get along. They don't even know we exist, Imber. If you continue down this path with her, maybe they will see that we are a people they have to contend with."

"Why would we want them to know we are even here?"

"Because they are doing something." His sister frowned, her eyes turning in a direction he couldn't see. "They're going to an area near where we hunt, very close to where the pod sleeps. We're not sure why."

There were more of the shells that she traveled in? He hadn't seen many in this area, but they were far from their hunting grounds. "What are they doing there?"

"None of us are sure. There's just strange bubbles always in the same area. The last time I went scouting, there were green rays coming out of the shells." His sister shuddered. "The light made me frightened, brother. I'm not sure they were there for a good reason."

That strange pit in his stomach was back. The same pit that happened when he smelled her fear.

Suddenly, he wondered if Alys hadn't been telling him everything. "I can ask her."

"You can speak with her?"

"She gifted me her language, and I gave her ours." The lights along his tail brightened in embarrassment as his sister thumped his tail with hers. "Sorry. I should have asked before I did that."

"Yes, you should have." She grabbed onto his cheeks and gave him a little shake before shoving him up into the current. She trailed along behind him as he made his way back toward their home. "I'm proud of you, though."

"I'm older than you, Virago. You don't get to be proud of me."

"Well, I'm bigger than you." His sister shrugged. "So maybe I get to be proud of my brother when I wish to be."

CHAPTER
Seven

STANDING in front of her father's office, Alys froze with her hand frozen and ready to knock on his door. She didn't want to do this. But she also didn't have a choice.

She'd heard the conversations. She knew what their people were planning to do, and she couldn't stand here and let it happen. Or at the very least, she needed confirmation that her father wouldn't actually let them destroy so much of the ocean.

She didn't even know if it would affect Imber and his people. But did it matter? Her people needed a safe place to live, but that didn't mean they got to destroy everything that stood in their way. That wasn't how the world should work. Not everything had to be a battle. Sometimes, it could just be a quiet ask and an understanding that of all the things that happened, there were people who were willing to help.

Still, she remained frozen. Afraid of what would happen if she asked her father to tell her the truth.

Because what if the truth was what she feared?

"Come inside, Alys," her father's warm voice called out. "I know you're out there."

Something melted inside her. Her father had always been a good man. He was the first one to show her the ocean and convince her to let it sink into her soul. He loved it just as much as she did, and he'd proven that to her countless times.

Of all people, he knew how important it was to maintain the glory and original beauty of the sea. He loved it. Deeply. They'd been on countless explorations together, just the two of them in his submarine where he named every single creature that they passed, every shell, even the currents that pushed their ship this way and that.

So she went into the room with her shoulders stiff and her jaw tight. Ready to argue for the place they both loved.

Her father sat at his desk, his glasses dangling from his neck while he poured over all the architectural designs that were likely for Alpha. His room was a mess, as always. Filled to the brim with objects they found on their dives, shells and coral and countless skeletons that he'd meticulously wire wrapped and then displayed. There was only one window in his room, but it didn't let in much light with the volcanoes like they were today. Instead, he lit the room with countless whale oil lanterns that turned everything orange and red.

He looked up at her, those eyes wrinkling at the corners because they always did when he saw her. His entire face lit up whenever his daughter walked into the room.

She remembered someone asking him about that once. And he said that his greatest discovery had nothing to do with the sea, but with the life he had made. Because no matter what he found, or what he made, his daughter would always be the first person who mattered.

Tears pricked her eyes. It was hard to think of her father as a bad man when he was the one who had been there for her. But she knew that he also wanted to make sure this city was everything that anyone had ever expected of him.

She loved him. Even through his faults. Even though maybe he was focused on this a little too much.

Sighing, she rubbed at her eyes and slumped into the chair in front of her father's desk. "Dad..."

"You seem upset."

"I've been listening through the walls," she muttered. "I overheard everything you and the General said to each other. And I... Dad. You can't do this."

Her father leaned back in his chair. She could see how hard it was for him to pull himself away from his work. Even when he looked at her, his eyes flicked to the small details on the pages in front of him. His mind didn't want to stop thinking about all the things that he needed to figure out. No matter how hard he tried to focus on her, he would always look first to his work.

It had been this way her entire life. Alys shouldn't feel so bad about it. When she was little, it was fun to work with him. She enjoyed going out to the sea and listening to him ramble about all the dreams he had. That he would be a great man who no one forgot.

But now, she saw the flaw in it. He was a man obsessed.

"Why?" she asked when he didn't reply to her. "Why do you want to ruin something so beautiful? Something you and I have dedicated our entire life to exploring?"

"We're not ruining all of it," he replied. But she could see the shadows in his eyes. Even he didn't believe his words. "Just a small section. Carving out an area for our people to live will not be easy."

"No, it won't. But I don't think the General is being honest with you. You don't need to have cameras and weapons pointed in every direction. What could possibly hurt us in the ocean?"

She knew what could hurt them. The undines were long and strong. They were powerful in a way no human could ever be, and she wasn't even all that confident her people could fight them off if they tried to attack. She knew, without a doubt, that should be a concern.

But she also respected Imber. She saw the beauty of his kind and understood that her people were trying to take over his home. They had to understand that there were people already there, and so the respect they had to have for the undines needed to come first.

She said none of this to her father. But when she looked at him, she could see a lie forming on his tongue so easily.

He...

Without thought, the words fell from her mouth. "You know."

Her father looked surprised. "What do I know?"

"About them." She shouldn't even be saying this.

What if he didn't know? What if she was letting her father know about this secret species and suddenly all of this might be her fault?

Could she trust her father with the knowledge that Imber's people existed? Would he run to the General and let that terrible man know that there were other things they had to worry about, and things that didn't have to do with structural integrity?

Her father slumped even more in his chair and then pinched the bridge of his nose. "Alys, I'm only going to ask this once, and I need you to tell me the truth. Where have you been going all these afternoons?"

A little bell of a voice in her head said that she should lie. He didn't need to know where she was going. What if this was a trick? A trap? What if they locked her up, and they refused to let her see Imber again?

But this was her father. And she loved him. Trusted him. Even though he had done some questionable things as of late, she knew, in his heart, he was a good man.

"I've been meeting with the sea," she replied quietly. She stared into his gaze, hoping he knew what that meant.

"Exploring?"

"Talking," she corrected. "And exploring, I suppose. But mostly talking."

She could see that he understood what she was saying. He knew that she meant she had conversed with the people under the sea and the spark of adventure in his eyes was so familiar it made her heart thud in her chest.

"How?" he asked.

"Beta."

"A translation chip? But we know nothing about their language."

Alys shifted uncomfortably in her chair. "I gave him a copy of Beta. And he brought it home with him."

"He?"

She nodded.

Her father let out a long breath. "So he brought Beta home and spoke with it?"

"For days on end, I assume. It's not a complete mapping of their language, and I did only have Beta create one before it turned itself offline because I didn't want anyone else getting their hands on the language without knowing what they might do with it." Strangely, she felt rather defensive about her plan. "I thought of everything, Dad."

"I can tell." He stood from his desk and then held out his hand for her to take. "I need you to see something."

That pit in her stomach continued to tighten as she followed him out of his office. Together, they left their home and walked down the boardwalks that brought them closer to the city. Not that it was much of a city anymore. They had a small gathering of the richer folks here, while everyone else had tried to live in the mountain towns.

It hadn't worked to save them. The air was even thinner up there, filled with ash and dust from the volcanoes. At least the storms didn't hit them like they hit the people on the coastlines, though. That's why they all lived in floating houses. Theoretically, their houses rode the waves that came in.

She'd still seen people lose their houses time and time again, though. And their lives.

Her father brought her to one of the homes that she'd always thought was storage and then pulled out a set of keys. Quickly, he unlocked the building while looking around them like someone might be following them.

Or perhaps that they would get in trouble if anyone caught them.

"Come on," he said, hastening her with his tone. "Let's go, Alys."

Together, they snuck into the darkness of the building. She was shocked to see what was beyond.

A room full of artifacts. Spears. Tools that surely were only used by Imber and his people. Strange looking skeletons that she quickly realized were one of the undines. The tail was so long, though. Longer even than Imber. There were so many creatures in here as well. Deep-sea species that she had never thought to see in her life.

There were even art pieces. Woven tapestries and necklaces like the one she hid underneath her thick sweater. So many pieces of his people's life, all held up in storage.

"What is this?" she asked. "Have you known about his people for a long time?"

"A very long time," her father replied. He strode into the center of the room, his hands tucked behind his back. "This is why the General wants to clear out everything around Alpha. He wants to make sure that none of them can get close to the city without him knowing."

"They aren't violent."

"Oh, but they are." With pursed lips and a furrowed brow, he turned his back to her and instead faced a spear that was longer than she was tall. "They have attacked us before. Most of the attacks were on the subs that have been scouting out an area for us to live. There are certain areas that they are much more protective of."

"Probably because that's where they live," she said. "Dad, can't you see this is wrong? We can't just move into where they have their homes and families. I don't care if Alpha's location is perfect. We can't build there."

"You cannot stop progress, Alys."

"Progress?" She felt nauseous even thinking of the word. "It's not progress, Dad. It's displacing a group of people who have never given us any trouble."

"We need a place to live. We need to go under the sea, and if we don't, we will all die." Her father's expression remained troubled, though. She knew he was bothered by this choice. "If we don't do this, then we may be the last humans alive on this planet. We will all be wiped out."

"There has to be another way."

"It's too late." Her father's shoulders rounded in, and she knew he would not change anything that he was doing. Not for her. Not for the undines. Not for anyone. "The plans have already been designed. I've already approved all the safety measures, and there is nothing I can do to stop it now. The General has what he needs to continue forward, with or without my help. But if I continue to help, then at least I can be assured that the city will be safely built. No one will cut corners. It won't flood or crack as we have always feared it would."

"You're going to destroy their homes," she said one last time. Tears dripped down her cheeks, and she tasted salt on her tongue. "These are people, Dad. They have a language, intelligence and kindness. Imber is..."

He interrupted her. "Imber?"

"That's his name."

"It is a good name. I hope he has been kind to you." Her father turned around, and she saw there were tears in his eyes as well. "Tell him to run, Alys. Or whatever it is that they do. Swim far away from here, because if he doesn't, then his people will die. The General will stop at nothing to get what he wants. You have little time left to convince them of that."

"Dad," she whispered, begging him to tell her this would not end the way she thought it would.

"When you see them, tell them I'm sorry." He shook his head after the words, as if he couldn't quite believe himself either. "If I could do something, I would stop it. Maybe if I had the foresight to see where this would have ended up. I know... I knew who the General was and what he would expect from my work. But this was the greatest design of my life and I got caught up in it."

"Dad, you have to stop them."

"I can't." A single tear dripped down her father's cheek. "Even if I tried, lovely girl, there is nothing I can do. I could rip my designs out of their hands and burn them, but that wouldn't stop them from building the city. It's too late. I was blind, and now I will hold this guilt for the rest of my life."

She took one step back. Then another. Another. Until there felt like an entire ocean between herself and her father.

He watched her movements with sad eyes and a heart that broke just like hers. "You'll tell them I'm sorry. Won't you, Alys? Warn them and then tell them that I am so, so sorry."

She didn't have it in her to say that she didn't think apologies meant anything when their homes were going to be destroyed. They would have to share an entire ocean with a species of creature that wanted to kill them, and she didn't know that Imber's people were equipped to handle people like hers. People with guns and technology that far outpaced their own.

Swallowing her tears, she bolted away from the building. She left her father in that treasure trove of discoveries that had led to this moment they both knew that there was no coming back from. As she slipped into her submarine, uncertain if anyone had seen her flee from that place, she couldn't get the General's face out of her mind.

"Beta?" she asked, waking up her droid to help her pilot the ship. "Take me to him."

CHAPTER

Eight

"IMBER!" The shout echoed through the water.

He was curled up on his small spiral of stones, worn soft and warm by the sea and his scales. He'd been dreaming about her. Alys. Because he was always dreaming about her.

Shaking the trailing fingers of the dream off, he sat up even as his gills flared around his neck and chest. He could smell it. The blood in the water that would soon draw predators to their home.

Blood? Why was there blood here?

Shooting out of his nest, he darted through the currents toward the smell. It didn't matter who was hurt or why they were calling for him, he had to go. His people needed him, and it didn't take even more than a second thought.

The sleep fell away from him and he saw a giant crowd in the center of their home. Men and women, all clustered around one of their own who laid bleeding on the central pattern. Coils of red plumed around the larger male who had been with the hunting party last night. There was a bright red blotch along his tail where something, or someone, had cut into it.

Not teeth. Not a round circular mark, as though he'd been

bitten by a shark or any other creature that lived in their homeland. It almost looked raw and ragged around the edges.

He'd never seen a wound like that before.

His sister darted toward him, her tail moving so quickly that her child nearly bounced free from the net. "Brother. You are well?"

"I'm fine." He clasped her arms, forcing her to look at him when she would have rushed off again. "What is going on?"

"They were attacked. You were supposed to be with that hunting party, and when you didn't come back with them, I thought..." Her eyes were wild with panic, and he knew that she'd been afraid he wouldn't return.

"Virago, I wasn't supposed to be with that hunting party. They sent me in the opposite direction yesterday with the others." He squeezed her forearms a little too hard, letting his claws sink into her skin in pinpricks of pain to anchor her. "I came back last night. With the others. We were all fine."

Her gills flattened against her neck and chest. "I... They were attacked, Imber. They were just swimming through the same paths we always do and something came out of nowhere. It... It..."

The male laying on the sands coughed out, "It burned."

"Poison?" he asked, because that was the only thing he could think of that would burn them. Burning was an unnatural sensation underneath the sea. Perhaps they had some kind of poison that hurt like when he had touched a puffer fish once when he was a child.

One of the females lifted a few of the male's scales around the wound and shook her head. "No. Burned." She looked up at the rest of them, her voice haunted. "Like the last homeland we left, where the water boiled from the land trying to take back the sea."

He remembered that, although he had been but a child. Imber remembered the red hot liquid that moved so slowly, but steadily approached them. He remembered the sound of popping water and the boiling that had sent so many creatures dashing toward them. He remembered how hard it had been to breathe.

The male sat up slightly, his breathing labored as he panted out the words. "They are coming here," he said. "They are coming to take our home."

His sister grabbed onto his arm, and Imber thought he felt a little faint.

Who was coming here?

"The achromos," the male said again, before he laid back on the sands, so still they all leaned forward to be sure his gills still fluttered.

Virago tugged at him, even though Imber wanted to check on the male to make sure he was still alive. Their pod was big. He didn't know the man personally but he should at least check. He felt responsible for this. He should have known they were coming. Surely Alys would have told him. He would have known that there was an attack about to happen.

Again, Virago yanked him away from the others. This time, he didn't have any choice but to follow her. He let her tug him away until no one could hear them.

Then she spun around. "You have to ask her to help us."

"I don't know what she can do."

"She's a female! Surely she has enough power that she can tell them to stop, or at least to move, so our hunting grounds aren't compromised!" Virago shook her head. "Beg her, if you have to."

"She's so small." He looked at his hands, as though he held her in them. "You've seen her, Virago."

"Only from a distance."

"She is smaller than any of our kind. I find it hard to believe that she has any power at all." Otherwise, this was partially her fault.

She could have stopped it if she had any power. And she hadn't. Which meant that maybe she didn't see the use in his people, or in him. And that hurt. That thought blistered through his very soul until he couldn't think or breathe through it.

"Brother," Virago said, her voice creased with concern. "We have to do something. We're the only ones who know one of their kind. Surely that means something. The sea would not send her to you without reason."

He nodded, even if his heart felt torn in two. "I will ask."

"Go to her now."

"The others will wonder where I am."

"I will tell them you went to scout out what is happening. That you will return with some kind of information that can help us." Virago tugged him close and pressed their foreheads together. He even felt his niece press her little forehead to his side before he was released. "Find out something we can use, Imber."

And so he fled from his people to the grove where he hoped she would wait for him. He didn't know how long it would take for her to come to him. They didn't usually see each other this time of the day, or even this time of the week. It might take days where he sat on the sands, waiting for her to tell him she had nothing to do with this.

Except, by the time he made it to the grove, there was already a metal shell waiting for him. He had only a few moments to be shocked before the top flew open so quickly the sound echoed around him.

Imber heard the muffled sound of his own name, shouted as she struggled to swim closer to him. He'd thought he would be angry at her. That he'd want to yell and scream, or ask what had she done? What had her people done?

But the moment he saw her, with those billowing skirts like the most delicate jellyfish belled around her, he couldn't be angry. All he wanted to know was that she was safe.

He'd flicked his fluke before he even realized he was moving. Then he was racing toward her, speeding through the water so quickly he swore it didn't even touch him before he had her gathered up in his arms. Her twin tails wrapped around his waist, holding him just as tightly as he held her.

They coiled around each other, tangling as best they could until he couldn't tell where he started and where she began. He held her close, breathing in her familiar scent and the hope that came with it.

"Alys," he breathed into her neck.

"I'm so sorry," she whimpered. "I'm so sorry, I didn't know. I didn't know what they were going to do, or that they knew about your people. I would have done something, I promise."

"You know now?"

"I know everything." Her entire body quaked in his arms, wracked with emotions as she struggled to speak through them. "I confronted my father. He's the main designers, and I'm sure that means nothing to you at all. I didn't know where they were going to build the city or that they knew you existed. All I heard at first was that they were going through with the design no matter who it affected, but I didn't ever think it would come to this."

He tugged her away from him, confused at what she was saying. And also because he wanted to look at her. He wanted to see the tears in her eyes and know without a doubt that she was as plagued by this as he was. "Alys. You have to tell me everything."

So she did.

Without hesitation.

He watched her purge the words with growing horror and a realization that nothing he or she did could stop what was going to happen. Women had no power in her world, at least not like in his. She couldn't tell them to stop building their new home, just like he couldn't tell his people to move. She would do whatever she could do, but that was so very little.

Her people were going to destroy his. They were going to take over ancient lands that had been in his family for generations. They would start a war with his people that wouldn't stop for generations to come, if it ever did.

A sudden premonition hit him like he'd been swallowed by a whale. They wouldn't stop fighting until one side was dead. Undines or humans, as she called herself. One of them had to die for the other to live.

He gathered her up again, tucking her head underneath his chin and holding onto her for all that he could.

This wasn't right. They were going to be fine. He would figure it out, or they would figure it out together.

"I'm so sorry," she said at the end of her story, still breathing hard. It was difficult to hear her through the mask she wore over her mouth. He wished he could take it off. He wished she could live under the water with him, just as he always wanted her to do.

"It's not your fault," he said, rubbing his hand up and down her back. "Although, I'll admit, I was hopeful you would be able to stop this."

"I don't know what to do." She leaned back, a strange grating noise coming out of her before he realized it was the sound of her sniffing. It had changed with her tears. "I just know that my father is part of it, and so it feels like I've been part of it as well."

"You couldn't have known."

"I should have done something earlier. Told you earlier." She shook her head, then pulled the mouthpiece off. He tried to ignore the mucus that she wiped away and then gently took out of the mouth piece before placing it back on. "My father said to apologize for him, and that he can't stop what's coming. Then he said to tell you that you should run."

"I don't know what this means."

"Leave. You should leave before they hunt you down." Big, sad eyes stared up at him, and he wanted to fight the world for her. "I think he might be right, Imber. I don't think there's a way for you to fight back against my people. I think you might all die if you tried."

"Your people would really kill us?"

She nodded miserably. "The General is an evil man. He sees nothing other than a land to conquer, and even if he could recognize that your people have been here long before we wanted to take your home, he wouldn't care. He sees it as a challenge."

"Part of me wants to say we will rise to that challenge." Imber raked his claws through her hair, gently tugging on a snarl that had already formed. "My people are fighters. I am gentle with you, Alys, but I am not always so gentle."

"I figured." Though she smiled and still traced his shoulders with her fingertips, he could sense that she hesitated. "I have studied the ocean my entire life. I know evolution and the changes of species through the centuries. I know the science. Nothing is born with so many weapons on their body, without being able to use them or having a good reason to use them. You are built like a predator, Imber. Don't think I ever forget that."

He took her hand in his and slid it down his arm. He used his own hand to force her to linger on the sharp points down the backs of his arms, then drew her closer to make her feel the spines down his back. Baring his teeth, he took her hand and touched her thumb to the sharp points of his teeth.

Throughout it all, she held her breath. Barely breathing at all as she allowed him to make her touch every single dangerous part of him.

And when he was done, when he was certain she had been frightened enough, he leaned down to press his lips against the very sensitive side of her neck. "I am a predator, Alys, but I am yours. In this time, in the next, in all the lives to come. I am yours. You never have any reason to fear me."

Her arms came down around him, her single heart thundering against both of his, and he knew in that moment that she understood what he was saying. She was safe.

He would keep her safe.

"What are we going to do?" she whispered, her voice thick with emotion. "We cannot stop them from building Alpha. I can't go back and tell my father that he needs to change something because he's not going to change. Our hands are tied. I cannot live with myself knowing that my people were the ones who cause yours so much pain. You don't deserve this. They don't deserve this."

"We will figure something out."

"It's your home, Imber." Her voice broke around the sadness and mourning that radiated throughout her entire body.

He could taste it in the water. Faint, because he realized her sadness tasted like the sea. Saltwater and a heavy brine that settled on his gills and dried into fractured pieces that dug into the sensitive membranes like sharp little claws.

Perhaps, even though he had always thought her weak, his Alys was stronger than he thought.

He drew back, pulling off her goggles so he could wipe away the tears. Usually she left these on in the water, saying her eyes needed the air. But when he went to put them back on her, she shook her head.

Alys let the goggles drop onto the sea floor. She took a deep breath, staring at him, and something settled between them. Some understanding that both of them had been fighting against, but they finally knew had to happen.

"Imber," she said, her voice strong and determined. "I want to help you. I want to help your people."

He nodded. Because, of course, this was the only way. "Don't go home this time," he said. "Stay with me."

CHAPTER
Nine

"STAY WITH ME," he said, as if it was that easy.

As if she could just stay underneath the water. As if she could just not go home and then live somewhere with him. It wasn't that easy, she wanted to tell him. Nothing was easy when she had to have air to breathe, and being under the water so much would eventually harm her. She couldn't just decide to stay here with him. That was a dream that would never work out in the end.

But then she thought about it. She let her mind wander through the possibilities and she thought...

Well.

Why not?

Sure, she couldn't live underwater forever. And she would run out of oxygen eventually, but that had to be fixable. She was the daughter of an inventor, and she could come up with something.

Glancing at the tubing attached to her face, and at the anchor of a ship she was connected to, she wondered if maybe she could figure out a way to lengthen the tube. If it was constantly in the air, maybe she could figure out some kind of pump system that would... she didn't know. Draw the air down to her?

It was a long shot. But still, without hesitation, she found herself saying, "I want to stay with you."

Like it was that easy. Like it was just a choice they both had to make. Like they could choose to do this together and the world would change with them.

His dark eyes lit up as if she'd given him the moon. His hands closed tighter around her waist, drawing her closer and closer to him until he pulled off her mouth piece and kissed her. And oh, it didn't matter then. Nothing mattered because he was kissing her, she was in his arms, and the ridiculous decision she had just made was for the both of them. Not just for herself.

A small prick at the side of her neck distracted her for a split second before his tongue swept into her mouth. Then nothing mattered. Because he had coaxed her to follow him, trailing her own tongue along the sharp points of his deadly teeth. He showed her again how deadly he was, how dangerous, and yet how gently he would treat her for the rest of her days if she trusted him.

Gods, she could love this undine. She could dedicate her entire life to making him happy just to feel the plush press of his lips to hers.

"I adore you," he said, his words eerily close to what she had just been thinking. "I want to keep you, Alys. I've wanted to keep you from the first moment I saw you. You are... everything. You know that, don't you?"

"Sure," she breathed against his lips. "I don't know if I'll ever believe that, but I want you. I want to stay. I want to be with you for the rest of my life, even if that's an insane thing to say."

And how...

How was she talking? How was she possibly saying that much when they both knew she needed air to breathe?

Leaning back, she felt panic flare a little too brightly in her chest for a brief moment. The mouthpiece wasn't on. Was this the few moments before she was going to drown? Had they finally made a mistake?

When that moment never came, heartbeat after heartbeat, she stared down at the mouth piece on the ocean floor. Oxygen still bubbled out of it, trailing up through the water in little iridescent bubbles that were so pretty to look at and yet so confusing at the same time.

"How?" she whispered, realizing that air was still exiting her mouth. Every time she spoke, a few bubbles popped out as well. That meant there was air in her lungs.

But...

The prick at the side of her neck. She watched Imber's eyes widen with brief horror before his clawed fingers touched the side of her neck. "I don't... I don't know how I did that."

She reached up her hand to touch his and realized there was a small tendril stuck to the side of her neck. Shifting her head from side to side, she realized she could almost feel it in her throat. Just a little hint that there was a foreign body somehow inside her.

She watched his chest rise and fall with a surprised breath, and she felt her own mimic his.

"Are you... breathing for me?" she asked, her voice little more than a whisper.

"I don't know."

It was the only explanation, and yet she didn't know how that was possible. He couldn't breathe for her underwater. It wasn't scientifically possible and yet, here it was.

She was underwater. With him. Not drowning even though her mouth piece had long been on the ground at her feet and... and...

"Wow," she whispered. "I didn't know we could do this."

"Neither did I." The shock had already faded from his eyes, though. He reached for her, his claws tangling in her long skirts as he dragged her closer to him. "But now you can be here without fear for your life. You can live under the water with me."

She knew that light in his eyes. It was the same expression he made when he wanted to kiss her. And it was always such a dangerous game they played when they kissed each other, knowing that she would have to eventually take a breath, or he would have to pinch her nose and force oxygen through her lips. They always knew they were only moments from her drowning.

But now?

They were safe.

Now he could hold her without fear. So he did. He dragged her into his arms, parting her legs around his hips with confident hands that had her arching into his grip.

It all suddenly hit her with all the weight of the sun. She was here, in his arms, underwater, and for the first time since she'd met him, she was safe. Safe to explore his body, his touch, the feelings that had been brewing for the few months that she'd known him. They had spent so much time together and she had been completely blind in the realization that she'd been carrying so much fear with her.

Every interaction, every touch, every moment that she got to see him, she was terrified.

What if she lost connection to her oxygen? What if she drowned right in front of him? What if someone followed her, or her ship broke down, or she disappointed him because she was weak and needed goggles and a mouth piece?

All of that faded away until there was nothing but her and him. Nothing but the man in front of her with heated eyes who wanted her.

He wanted to touch her. To hold her. To kiss her because he knew, for the first time, it was safe to do so.

She would be an idiot to not take advantage of every second.

She grabbed onto his shoulders and yanked him to her. She could feel the slight huff of surprise that echoed through his body because it also puffed air into her lungs. But the flexing of his claws against her spine, or the way he grabbed handfuls of her skirt before stopping himself, all of it told her just how close he was to losing his control as well.

"I want you," she moaned against his lips. "I don't care how or why this has happened. I want you."

And maybe, just maybe, he wanted her as much as she did him.

Like she'd unleashed a shark, he descended upon her. She only had a few moments to realize they were sinking to the sands before her back hit them. A plume of sand covered her vision for a brief moment before his gills fluttered hard enough to push it all away from her. He loomed over her, a dark shadow with a frame of the sea behind him.

"I have wanted to taste you for such a long time," he growled, his voice low and guttural.

She didn't know what to say. She didn't even know how he would taste her, but... Sure. If that's what he wanted to do. Nodding frantically, she wrapped an arm around his neck and kissed him again. Arching into him, wanting whatever he would give her. "Then taste me."

He groaned, his body going rigid under her touch. "We are not a gentle people, Alys."

"I don't want gentle."

"I don't know how to do this the way your people do, maybe..."

She leaned away from him, a full-blown glare on her face. "Do you want me?"

"*Yes.*" The word wrenched out of him like she had pulled it out of his heart. "More than anything."

"Then touch me how you want. Taste me how you want. I don't even know what that means, but I'm telling you that nothing you do will feel wrong." She kissed him again, sweeter this time, but with no less desire. "No one has done this before, Imber. I think it's safe to say that anything we do will be new for the both of us."

He shook his head, gliding his lips over hers. "I don't want to hurt you."

"I'll tell you if it hurts."

She didn't think any of it could hurt. All of his touches had felt like little lightning bolts for weeks now, and surely he knew that? He had to know...

Then all thought fled from her mind.

He'd leaned down and dragged his tongue up her throat. She had that tongue in her mouth more times than she could count now, but she hadn't realized it was ridged. There were bumps there, like little suction cups that moved up and down the sensitive skin of her neck. Shivering, a little moan escaped her lips before she could catch it.

"Good?" he asked.

"Yes," she whimpered. "Don't stop."

But he wouldn't. Because he was already molding her body with the palms of his hands. Broad and wide, he could fit her entire breast and some of her rib cage in a single grip, but oh, it felt amazing. He watched her as he touched her everywhere. Lingering on the spots that made her gasp.

His thumbs brushed against her nipples, working them into stiff peaks that sent little bolts of energy between her legs. She couldn't get enough air from him, dragging on the tentacle attached to her neck like it was a drug. Especially when his hands smoothed down her belly, then gradually started lifting handfuls of skirt up her legs.

Inch by inch, he feasted on the sight of her.

"You will tell me more about these tails soon enough," he grumbled, lifting one of her legs high to nip at the delicate skin behind her knee. "But first, I need to know where this taste is from."

"Taste?" she asked, almost delirious with need.

The gills around his neck fluttered. "I can taste the water, Alys. I can taste you."

Oh god, was he suggesting that he could taste her on the water? Like the actual taste of her arousal was... was...

He pushed her skirts up high and then suddenly he was between her legs. The featherlight touches of his gills fluttered against her inner thighs, the sensation nearly sending her into a spiral of pleasure before those ridges of his tongue slid through her folds.

She arched into him, her entire body seizing around the sensation of that touch.

"Pain?" he asked, pausing between her legs even as those gills slid between her thighs.

He was touching her with his gills. They were soft and so gentle. Even though the touch was otherworldly, they fluttered so perfectly around her that she could only choke out words that maybe sounded like, "Don't stop."

The low growl that vibrated against her was nearly enough to send her careening into the hardest orgasm of her life. She was so glad it didn't, though, because she wanted to savor this moment.

He turned all his attention between her legs and feasted. For all that he had no experience with a human, he made up for it in sheer enjoyment. The noises he made, the grunts and groans of pleasure every time he licked over her clit or felt her thighs clamp down harder around his head, it all made the pleasure inside her coil higher and higher.

She glanced down, seeing black claws ripping through her skirts and his tail lashing behind him as he ground himself into the sand and she almost couldn't take it.

She wanted... needed... more. Him. Everything. She wanted to see him, feel him stretching her, pushing her to a point where there was no return. She wanted to know what it felt like to not just be devoured by an undine, but consumed.

Grabbing onto his hair, she pressed him to the perfect spot as his tongue lashed against her. "Yes, Imber, right there."

He groaned, a long, low word that sounded like a curse. "You taste so good," he growled before plunging his tongue deep inside her.

And what a long tongue it was. She arched her body, riding his tongue like she would his cock as he pistoned it in and out of her pussy. She was glad they were underwater or she might have heard the obscene sounds of how wet she was and how hard she rode him, but then stars sparkled beneath her eyes.

He bent his tongue, pressing against something inside her and all those little suction cups gripped onto her and she exploded.

Every muscle in her body locked up tight. She couldn't see. Couldn't breathe. Couldn't do anything other than hold on to him and hope she made it out of this alive, because she thought maybe she wouldn't.

Eventually the clenching muscles gave, and she slumped down onto the sand. There really wasn't enough air for her to breathe, but she felt him breathe a little harder for her so she could at least get her heart to beat a little slower. It wasn't easy, though. Not when she was so limp in his arms.

He braced himself over her, that long, dark tongue licking his lips as though he couldn't stand wasting a single taste of her.

"I'd like to do that again," he said, his voice still thick and ragged. "Soon."

"Yeah, when I can breathe again," Alys replied, then giggled. "I don't... I don't think I can move."

"Good, you don't have to." Imber smoothed her hair away from her face. "For now, I should get you somewhere safe."

She shook herself free from the post orgasm haze, reminding herself that technically they weren't safe yet. They were still in the ocean, likely still near the dig site for Alpha. They had a lot of things to do, and she couldn't just snuggle into him when all she wanted was to return the favor.

"But what about you?" she asked, drawing her fingers down his lips. She couldn't stop touching him. Not after that.

He grinned, nipping at her lips. "Soon, little one. Soon. But first, we have to do something about your shell."

"My shell?" She frowned before realizing he was looking at her ship. "Ah. Right. That is a problem."

One that was easy to fix, even if it meant that she would have to break her father's heart a little. It made her own heart break, but she hoped he would see it as a sign.

He was the only one who knew she was close with the undine. He was the only one who knew that she wasn't alone in the ocean.

She made quick work of it. She couldn't even let Beta know that she was going to be okay, or the little droid would have to tell them. So she directed Imber. "Rip off the front glass, if you can. There's a red button on the top panel. It's an emergency protocol that will make it go home on its own. It should be able to do so even with all the water damage."

He gave her a look, clearly unimpressed that she thought he couldn't rip off the panel. She watched with wide eyes as he made it look almost easy. He tore the glass off like it wasn't held down by industrial strength bolts that were then welded onto the metal.

He could have ripped the whole thing open like a tin can if she asked him to do that. And somehow, that was thrilling more than it was terrifying.

When it was all said and done, there was very little to do other than rub at the faint ache in her chest. They were still connected by that tentacle, far enough to be an arm's length away, and that was all. So when he gathered her close, it felt only natural to move even closer.

"Come home with me?" he asked.

She found it was hard to do anything other than nod against his chest and mourn the loss of her old life. Even as she felt a spark of excitement to see her new one.

CHAPTER

Ten

NERVES CHURNED in his belly as he swam her away from the grove. He had never thought this would be possible, let alone that he would bring Alys back to his family.

But no part of him regretted asking her. The only thing he had to be nervous about was whether or not they would let her stay.

He thought they would. Maybe. His people were suspicious of hers, considering the attack that had just happened and the fact that they were going to be faced with more attacks soon. But maybe, just maybe, she could win them over.

Imber tried to prepare himself for the inevitable. Someone would try to hit her or scratch her. They would want to take their pound of flesh for what her people had done to his. Though they were likely owed that, he didn't want to see her harmed. She wasn't the one who had burned his pod mate. She wasn't the one who had designed this new city of theirs.

Perhaps he should hope that his sister found them first. Virago would be a much larger shield for his Alys while Imber tried to calm everyone down.

Come to find out, he didn't need to worry in the slightest.

The first moment they could see his home, the swirling

patterns of stones marking the way to their nests, they were spotted. The undines rose from their nests, all of them swimming toward him in a wall of colorful creatures that likely terrified her with their movements. They rose out of the ocean and came for her, long claws outstretched and their dark eyes wide.

He tried to see them as she did. They were rather monstrous compared to her, although they were his family and friends. They looked like him. Alys tightened her tails around him, holding onto his shoulders and squeezing a little harder as she tried to straighten up.

He wanted to tell her to be brave. He wouldn't leave her side, even if they tried to tear her from him.

But he didn't have to worry about any of it. The moment the first of his people reached for her, she went without question. She untangled her tails from her, brushing her hair back away from her face, and reaching out for the giant female as well.

Aluo was one of the largest females in his pod, if not the largest. He still remembered watching her grow as they were children and being ridiculously intimidated by her size. She had ended up nearly double his size, and her broad shoulders with stacks upon stacks of muscles made her a formidable opponent. He'd seen many males die as she mated with them.

But Alys didn't even flinch. She touched her fingertips to Aluo's, a smile on her face as she looked at how large in comparison the hand was to hers. And then, with a surprising movement, she pressed Aluo's fingers against her forehead.

How did she know?

How did she so easily fit into his people without question and make a movement that was clearly meant with respect? He watched Aluo's expression change from one of suspicion to softness, and then they were swarmed by the People of Water.

So many of them dove all around him, darting through the currents as they tried to touch her. Some of them ran their claws through her hair, others touched gentle fingers to the bottom of her feet. So many people, all trying to catch a glimpse of the strange creature he had brought to them.

She did what she could to endure their curiosity. Imber could see she was getting nervous, though. Most of that had to do with when one of his people got too close to the short cord holding them together. If they ripped out his tentacle, she was too deep underwater to reach the surface before she would drown.

Flicking his tail, he moved closer, gripping her hand in his so she wouldn't float too far from his side.

"I've got you," he murmured, dragging her a little closer as yet another of his people caught hold of her foot. "I won't let anything happen."

"I know," she whispered, squeezing his fingers.

But her eyes were still a little wider than he'd like to see. Even though she put on a brave face, he knew this was overwhelming.

Finally, the crowd parted and his sister swam through it. Virago looked particularly exhausted today. Or maybe that was just the little one attached to her hip that was wriggling and reaching out for him with grabbing hands.

Soon, he would hold his niece again. But right now, he wanted them all to see that she wasn't a threat.

"Brother," Virago said, her voice pitched loud so that everyone could hear her. "You have brought one of the achromos to our home."

"I did."

"The dangers they have caused in our waters are reason enough to not bring her here. So please, explain to us all why you hold on to her like a mate."

His sister already knew the answer, but the others didn't. This was her way of telling him to weave a tale that would make them all relax. A tale that would convince them to let her stay.

So they all sank down toward the sands and the spiraling stones. He kept her in his arms, wrapping his tail around her so she was as tangled with him as he was with her. It was a sign that she was his mate, but also that he wouldn't let anyone else touch her.

Then he told them their story.

Every word warmed him to the core. He had chosen correctly. Alys had proven herself to be good and wise with every turn. Her adventurous spirit was a captivating part of the story, as was her bravery when she first faced him down. He left out the parts where they had explored each other's bodies, namely because he didn't know what to say about it.

She hid a treasure trove between her twin tails, one that tasted as sweet as the oysters that he harvested for his pod to eat. He'd never look at one the same again.

Even though his grip had loosened around her as he spoke—as he was less concerned with someone taking her from his arms—she had taken to stroking his tail. He knew there were many who watched her do so. They were pleased with how easily she showed him affection, and even more pleased that she wasn't disgusted with the touch.

They didn't know, of course, that she could understand every word he said. At least until he told them about the device she'd created and affixed to his ear.

"She can understand us?" Virago asked, her voice loud and booming, even though she already knew this detail of the story.

"Just as I can understand her."

Alys glanced between the two of them, clearly sensing the tension in the water. But then again, she didn't need to be a shark to be able to smell that. "If I may?"

He saw a few of the others wince at the sound of her clipped voice. "Quietly, little one. Your voice is..."

"Grating?" she replied, trying not to laugh.

Imber nodded. He didn't want to insult her or her people any more than she would endure living here with him. But he supposed... Well, the truth had to come out at some point. "It is very high pitched."

"Ah." She brought her words down to barely a whisper and

then slowed them down even further. "I am the only one who can understand you. Please tell them that the devices I created were only so we could speak with each other. They were only a one time creation. The droid that made them, Beta, it's with my father. I don't think I could make them again, and my people certainly cannot."

He repeated the words to his sister, making sure that he said everything that she wanted his sister to know. And when he was finished, Virago gravely nodded.

He saw the expression on her face. It was one of sadness, and he already knew he wouldn't like what she was about to say.

"I think it would be best if we keep it that way." She even looked Alys in the eyes as she said it. "I am sorry that we will not be able to converse easily, new sister. But your people cannot have a way to know our language, and I refuse to put anyone else in danger because of it. The risk is too great."

Alys nodded before looking up at him. "I agree with her."

"Are you sure?" It broke his heart to think she would never truly be part of his people. She would be able to understand them fully, but, like a pet, they would never be able to understand her.

"It's technology I don't think my people should ever get their hands on," she confirmed. "Your sister is right."

So he repeated the words and then answered any questions his people might have.

How did they meet?

Where did she come from?

What were the small flippers on her tails? Why did they have notches in them?

They reached for her hands again, touching the long funnels between her fingers where there should be a membrane. And she let them. His little Alys answered every question without fail, even when she yawned and yanked the air out of him so quickly with the movement that he had to pound on his chest.

Finally, he couldn't take it anymore. This was the first time he'd had her in his world, and they were both exhausted. His people would have more time to ask them questions, but for now, "We're both tired," he interrupted the newest person asking her questions. "I think I should get her to bed."

"To bed?" his sister asked. "In your nest?"

He hadn't thought that far ahead. His nest was one of the many that didn't have any cover. It would be a miracle if either of them got any sleep with so many people staring at her. He wouldn't put it past the more curious younglings to sneak a touch while she was resting.

Rolling her eyes, Virago gestured behind her. "Take mine for the night, brother. Perhaps then you will have some semblance of rest."

"I couldn't. Your daughter—"

"Will be fine with me in your nest tonight." She grinned, sharp teeth flashing in the dim light. "Take your achromos to my nest, brother. Make sure she has good dreams there, yes?"

Alys would understand the words, although he wasn't sure she knew what his sister meant. Good dreams were only for those who had earned them. His sister had essentially told him to work hard to give her a restful night, which meant... his sister couldn't possibly be suggesting what he thought she was suggesting.

Embarrassment heated his cheeks, and he gathered Alys up in his arms before she could ask what his sister meant. He would not explain in front of everyone that his sister was highly inappropriate.

Drifting through the water, away from his people, to where they were finally going to be alone again, it eased something in his chest. Though he adored his people, he hadn't realized just how much he wanted to be alone with her.

They had always had their own time together. That kelp grove had been their haven, far away from anyone else that might look in on them. And he didn't want to lose that.

He'd liked it being just the two of them. Without that, what did they have? Just a lot of responsibility and weight on their shoulders. Too much stood between them, and being here reminded him of that.

"Imber?" Alys asked, her hands braced on his chest as he swam them toward the covered nest. He stopped in front of it, hesitating.

The inside smelled like his sister and his niece. There were little toys hanging from the covering above them and it was so... his sister. He couldn't sleep with her here. It wasn't right. It wasn't them.

"I think I know a better place," he said, bumping her forehead with his. "You trust me?"

"As long as a shark doesn't try to eat me in the middle of the night."

"There aren't that many sharks in the ocean."

"Says you." She leaned back in his arms as he swam them in the opposite direction. "Have you seen all the sharks in the ocean?"

He snorted. Somehow this woman made him laugh even when he was exhausted. "No."

"Then you don't know that there aren't that many. Maybe they're all waiting in the shadows for you to drop your guard." She crossed her arms over her chest, letting him carry her weight with so much trust it humbled him. "I think you have a lot to learn, Imber."

"About my own home?"

"About everything." A warm spark in her eye nearly set him on fire. "About me."

Ah, and there it was. The warm scent of her in the water that turned his entire body into pure muscle and anticipation. He wanted her. He could still taste her, even though he'd tried very hard to ignore that fact.

Now, as he swam them toward a coral grove with a winding labyrinth to get to the center, he had all the time in the world to explore her. "You aren't too tired?" he asked, making sure that he was taking care of her at the least. "We can still rest."

"I've been trying very hard to be polite to your family, but I haven't stopped thinking about you since the moment you touched me in the kelp forest." She looped her arms around his neck, drawing him down to press a lingering kiss to his gills. And oh, he fluttered.

He fluttered so hard that he could see the sand moving from how hard he shifted the water around them. He was creating a current all of his own because of how badly he wanted her.

But first, he really should tell her how they were different. Or at least, he assumed there were differences. After all, she looked nothing like the females of his species. She didn't have a single tail. There wasn't a small slot in the front like there would be for his females. And he didn't have to wrap his tail around her to hold her in place.

She'd stayed right where he wanted her. Almost as though the weight of him was welcome as he'd feasted upon her flesh. The experience with her had been entirely about pleasure and without an ounce of pain.

"I am..." He cleared his throat. "Not like your kind."

"I know," she replied with a gleam in her eyes. "And I'm looking forward to seeing how different you are, Imber."

CHAPTER
Eleven

SHE KNEW that he was worried. She'd been worried when he first touched her, because she knew how different they were. Alys had been afraid to disappoint him. She had worried he might see the differences and find her ugly.

But he hadn't. Imber had looked at her and reacted like she was a goddess and he was the lucky bastard who got to spend a few minutes with her. That reaction, more than anything else, gave her the courage to take control.

If he needed her to prove that she wasn't afraid, and in fact elated to have this moment with him, then she would happily do so. Nothing would distract her from this. Especially now that he had laid her out, surrounded by a rainbow of coral, and he was right here. Ready for her to do whatever she wanted with him.

Biting her lip, she eyed the nervous expression on his face before deciding she knew what to do.

"I've been waiting a long time for this," she whispered, planting her hands against his chest and giving him a little shove. He didn't fight her.

Imber rolled onto his back, allowing her to straddle him and to gently move their connection to her right. She wanted that cord within sight, but she also didn't want to think about it. Distractions had no place here.

Then she forgot about the dangers of being underwater and instead focused on the handsome creature splayed out underneath her. She skated her fingers over his chest, letting her fingers dip into the hollows where muscles created shadows. He was warmer than she expected. Normally, he was a rather chilly creature to touch.

But every time she pressed down on a new muscle, or moved farther down his body, he seemed to radiate even more heat. As she watched, the gills on the side of his neck flared out, shaking just a bit with nerves or perhaps with want.

"Alys," he murmured, licking his lips as his eyes went even darker. "I don't know that you'll like what you find."

"Hm?" She leaned down and flicked one of his rib gills with her tongue. "I don't know why or how you're still thinking."

Although he didn't seem to hear the words she said. Because he was arching into her, his spine curving as her lips and tongue descended on one of the most sensitive parts of his body. He shook against her, this massive creature quaking in her arms all because of her soft lips and darting tongue.

She could get used to this. Having him come apart underneath her was surprisingly empowering.

Perhaps this was how he'd felt when she lay beneath him as well. Writhing in the sands because he'd brought her to such an incredible peak that she'd seen stars.

Again she hummed, and his tail thudded hard against the sand as she slid her lips a little lower. Tracing the lines of his abs with her tongue and then biting down on his side with a sharp little nip that had him hissing out a breath. She looked up at him, one eyebrow raised as he clearly tried to get control of himself.

"What are you doing?" he rasped.

"Do your people not do this?"

"I don't know what you're even trying to do." His hands clenched in the sands, and she wondered if he was trying to stop himself from yanking her up to his face. "I told you already, Alys. My people's mating dance is brutal and painful. Especially for the male."

She let out a little mewl that made her question if she'd even made the noise. The pitying sound was so teasing and so... erotic. "Poor Imber. I should make that up to you."

His dark eyes flashed with desire, and his voice deepened. "Just how are you going to that, little one?"

She could explain it to him, but she wanted to show him. Alys moved down his body, allowing his tail to slither between her legs. His scales dragged over her folds and the slight abrasion had her shuddering. But right now wasn't about her. All she had to do was find his... well, hopefully he had....

Her hands smoothed over a part of his scales that didn't feel like the rest. She wasn't sure why it felt different. Perhaps it was that it felt a little hollow compared to the rest of his scales. But she knew right away that this must be the area she was looking for.

She could only hope he had a cock like a human. Things would be fine if he didn't. She'd miss certain aspects of that but... her fingers grazed over the area and then he was there. All at once, sliding out from behind the scales and revealing that he definitely had a cock.

In fact, he had two.

"Two," she whispered, taken a little aback by the discovery.

He looked down his body at her, still laid out on the sands like a banquet she could feast upon whenever she wanted. And he looked... nervous. "Is that a surprise?"

"Definitely." She needed to maybe not stare at him with such wide-eyed shock. But two of them.

And they were huge, lying right on top of the other. Long and tapered, at the very least, so she could imagine they would go in rather easy. The tip was significantly thinner than the rest of him, and all smooth. Very little texture, and ridiculously wide at the base. She wasn't entirely sure it was logical that she *could* take all of him but the more she stared, the more she wanted to try.

Perhaps she should ease into it. Perhaps she should just try to see where her original plan got them. So, making eye contact with him and a little smile, she licked the top one from the base to the tip.

She didn't miss the nervous expression before he slammed his head back against the sands. Of course, that would make sense. He'd said his people had a rather violent sexual experience whenever they were together, so it made sense that he'd likely never experienced this before. A blowjob wasn't conducive to pain.

Licking him again, she gently slid the tip of him into her mouth and swirled her tongue around it. She took her time learning what made him gasp and writhe against the sands. Mostly because she didn't know his anatomy, and also because she liked having him at her mercy.

His claws dug into the sand. The fluke of his tail slapped against the ground multiple times before she felt him wrap the very tip around her leg. Almost as though he wanted to coil around her like a snake, but knew that if he did that, she might stop what she was doing. And he couldn't let her stop what she was doing. Not when he wanted it so badly.

It was different from any of her other sexual experiences. He wasn't built like a human, but she wasn't built like him. The more she licked and touched, the more she thought this might actually be possible.

"Alys," he groaned. "You have to stop. I'm going to—"

She didn't want to stop.

So she didn't.

In fact, she sucked even harder. Squeezed with her hands a little tighter, just to see what would happen. What did he taste like?

Then his cock jumped against her tongue and suddenly he was spurting into her mouth. Not eggs, as she had the briefest flicker of fear that he might. But a rather umami flavored seed that coated her mouth with a not so unpleasant flavor at all.

When she opened her eyes, the iridescent liquid had escaped her lips. It floated up between them, shimmering like a rainbow, and she had the strange sensation that it might be the prettiest thing she'd ever seen before.

Then he reached down for her, gently dragging a claw tipped finger over her bottom lip. He looked at her like she was a goddess. And maybe, just maybe, she was a little.

"I didn't realize your mouth could do that." He pressed a little harder against her lips, forcing her to open her mouth. "I don't think I'll look at it the same way again."

She licked the tip of his finger. "Well, I had to return the favor."

Those eyes darkened, and he sat up. Pulling her with him, he wedged her in his lap and she felt how hard he still was. Impossibly. She hadn't thought...

With a gasp, she froze as he lifted her just enough to put the head of his bottom cock against her entrance.

"Wait," she whispered. "You can still..."

"Alys, I have two of them for a reason." Those dark eyes met hers with an intent stare. "As long as you still wish to..."

"Yes!" she blurted a little too quickly. "It's just, normally, there's a refractory period."

"A what?"

"Men don't stay hard where I come from." She reached down and touched the top cock that was still half hard. "There's some benefit to having you around, I see."

The crooked grin on his face was enough to send a rush of heat between her legs. "Oh, Alys, you have no idea how much you're going to like having me as your mate."

She should have argued that he wasn't her mate. That the term was a little too barbaric for her, but she didn't. Instead, she reveled in the thrill the words sent shooting through her body as his tail suddenly undulated behind her. He looped it around her waist, locking her in place even as the rest of it created a comfortable brace for her back.

Then he flexed all those muscles in his tail and the head of him slid inside her. She felt her mouth drop open as she made a little sound of surprise. Even the head of him, and she'd had that in her mouth, was so *big*.

His face contorted with pleasure, those fangs bared as he wedged himself a little deeper, drawing back only to push in a little farther the next time. He eased himself inside her, slowly working over and over again with so much patience that it made her heart race.

Throughout it all, he whispered encouragement.

"Alys, yes. Breathe, you beautiful woman. Breathe for me, love. Look how well you take me."

She hadn't realized just how much she enjoyed hearing the deep sound of his voice, and the praise that dripped off his tongue so easily.

He leaned down, his long tongue wrapping nearly entirely around her breast as the tip teased her nipples into hard points that ached for more of his touch. More of him. She needed him, wanted him, and then she felt him bottom out inside her. He groaned, and the sound mixed with the whimper of need that made her throat tighten.

"Move," she said. "Please, I want to feel you."

It was all he needed. He drew back and slammed inside her so hard she felt her teeth rattle, but it didn't matter. It was everything she had asked for and more. What he lacked in texture, he made up for in stretching her so wide it was hard to breathe sometimes.

Every slam inside her, every slow glide, it brought her closer and closer to the orgasm she chased. Needing. Wanting. Aching for what he could give her until... until...

He reached between them and pressed his other cock against her, rubbing it with every stroke against her clit. The sensation of him, of being filled by him and still having more than she could touch and taste if she wished. It was too much. Both cocks were so hard now and he was touching her with both of them.

She clamped down on him, so tight he was forced to freeze inside her. A low growl echoed through his chest, fluttering his rib gills against her as he arched. It was so much, so perfect, everything she needed.

Alys had always closed her eyes when she came. It was a natural response, she'd always thought, sealing the emotions inside her because she couldn't look at the other person while she felt such pleasure in her body. But this time, she kept her eyes open. She watched the monstrous being inside her come, and he was glorious.

Every muscle bulged with his release. He looked every bit the monster that she knew he could be, and yet, she wanted him even more. The sight of him losing himself completely inside her, the feel of the hot gush between her thighs, it only made her come even longer.

He was perfect. He was everything she hadn't realized she'd been looking for until this moment, with his cock still twitching inside her and his already spent cock between them.

This wasn't traditional. She couldn't even claim it was normal.

But it was what she wanted, and she was so happy.

Imber's tail shifted underneath her, dragging her limp body even closer to his arms so he could wrap her up in him. He let the ocean hold both of them, buoyant and comfortable as they slowly spiraled down from an orgasm that had shaken her to her very core.

Breathing hard still, she tried to suck as much air as she could from their connection. He was breathing just as ragged as her, so it was rather easy to catch her breath. It also connected them even more, because she knew what his body felt like. How hard it was for him to breathe right now, and how his heart thundered against hers.

Or two of his hearts, she supposed as she pressed her hands against both of the thuds and smiled up at him. "Still with me?"

"For as long as you'll have me," he breathed, pressing a kiss to the top of her head and coiling her a little tighter in his grip. It meant that he slid out of her, but she was so wrapped in him that it didn't matter.

Breathing together, safely tucked into the sands and surrounded by so much coral, it was like she was in a dream. As though she'd slipped into her greatest desire and stayed there.

All the worries bled out of her body until she only had him and her. Curled around each other, the softness in her heart spread into him.

She felt the little sigh that rocked through her body as he tucked her underneath his chin and they both slipped into sleep. There were no words for what they had just done.

There was only the knowledge that they were safe with each other. And as she drifted off into sleep, she realized she didn't just feel safe with him physically.

Because she knew, without question, that he would also be careful with her heart.

CHAPTER
Twelve

HE DIDN'T WANT to wake her, so he didn't.

Imber laid there with her draped across his chest, trying to keep his breathing slow and quiet so she wouldn't wake herself just because of the way he was breathing. He wanted her to sleep for as long as she needed.

She'd earned her rest. Even now, he could feel his cocks twitching at the memory. He would love nothing more than to wake her with a slow stroke between her legs, to see her eyes widen with desire and passion.

But he wasn't an animal, as much as his form suggested that he might be. He couldn't wake her up with expectations. Instead, he would allow her to continue to sleep because she trusted him. And this was enough for now.

Her hair laid across his shoulder, the silken feel of it so different from his own people's. Her tails on either side of his hips made him worry she might wake a bit uncomfortable. At some point during the night, she had straightened them. When he noticed they drifted a bit in the currents, every time she stirred a bit in her sleep, he'd wrapped his tail around her. Giving her a brace against the sea she wasn't yet used to.

Then she'd fallen into such a deep sleep, he almost felt as

though he was breathing for her. Of course, he was, but he worried that she wouldn't be breathing at all if he hadn't been pushing air into her lungs with every deep breath of his own.

He just worried in general. She wasn't built to live in the ocean like he was, and there were many reasons for him to be afraid for her. It hadn't even been a full day yet since she'd been in the water, and already her fingertips were... wrong.

He was used to seeing them smooth like his own skin. But he'd lifted her hand to his lips just a few hours ago and noticed that her skin was waterlogged and wrinkly.

Wrong. It was wrong. He needed to ask her what was happening to her while she was in the water, and what they could do to stop it from happening.

A ripple of movement caught his attention above their heads. A shadow passing in front of the sun, a long tail and a sleek body that was designed for hunting. His sister. He would know Virago in any shape or form, at any distance.

Why would she be coming out here? Hadn't she been the one to tease him that he should take his mate and attend to her? Frowning, he closed his arms a little more tightly around his little achromos.

A low sound echoed through his chest, not quite loud enough to wake Alys but enough for his sister to hear. And she did. Quickly changing directions, his sister dove toward them. When she was closer, he could smell the fear drifting off her body in waves.

"What happened?" he asked, noting that her daughter was not attached to her hip.

"The achromos have come." Virago's eyes skated over Alys, curled up in his arms, and she hadn't even stirred yet. "You've made quick work of your mate, I see."

"Virago," he growled.

"We knew they were coming for our home, brother. We knew they were going to arrive sooner rather than later."

"Where is my niece?"

"Safe, with the others. We need to gather all the things that we can, and those who were too weak to do so have already moved. I tried to give you time with her, but there is no more time left." Virago's gills spread wide around her face and ribs, and he knew then that the situation was dire.

They weren't ever getting their home back. It was just like Alys said. Her people didn't care what they were doing to the ocean. This was the spot they had chosen, and they would destroy it.

Alys stirred against him, her tails squeezing tight as she slowly came awake. She took a deep breath, sucking all the air out of his lungs in what he thought might be a yawn before she blinked her eyes open and looked up at him.

She was so adorable. Tucked up against him, all soft and warm and completely unaware of what was happening. Her nightmares were so far away in the dreaming world, but she had no way of knowing they had chased her into the real world.

"Good morning," she said, her voice a little raspy with sleep and so quiet he almost didn't hear her.

"We have to wake, my wave song."

"No sleeping in today, hm?"

Virago's voice cut through their quiet conversation. "Your people have come to destroy ours, Alys of the achromos. I know this is not what you want to hear after the night you had with my brother, but you are able-bodied. If nothing, you can carry whatever we need."

He felt his hearts turn over in his chest as her eyes widened. With a sharp slap of her hands against his chest, she sat up. Her hair billowed in front of her face and she had to shove all the golden locks out of her way to glare at his sister. "What do you mean?"

He repeated the words to his sister. And Virago sighed. "I mean there are metal beasts clearing the ocean. They approach our home and we need all the help we can get to move out of their way."

Alys looked at him, then back at his sister. She spoke to him, but he had a feeling the words were for Virago as well, if his sister could have understood her. "I'm so sorry. I knew they were going to be coming, but I didn't know it would be this soon. I thought you all had more time."

He squeezed her thighs before unraveling their bodies. But he couldn't bring himself to let her go, and kept an arm around her waist as he swam them up to his sister. "There was nothing you could have done, Alys. Like you said, none of us could stop this."

His heart broke in the silence that followed. They swam through the currents and the waves, and he knew he was returning to what would be a very sad scene. His people had to flee from their homes. The places they had lived for years on end, even if they had only recently come back to these hunting grounds. He wasn't even sure where they would go now. But they would find somewhere they were welcome.

Alys, on the other hand, seemed to take all this to heart. He could feel her growing more and more angry. The scent of it filled his gills.

These were her people, and she was deeply unhappy with them. He wouldn't be surprised if her anger spilled onto others as well. There were a lot of people who were ready to be angry.

Now, all he could do was hope that he could control the situation.

It was no surprise that he couldn't.

The moment they all crested the rise that brought them to his home, he could see the metal demons in the distance. They weren't just scouting this time, they were destroying everything in their way. Countless of his people gathered whatever items they could. A few of them darted past, their arms already laden with food, tapestries, even a few of the stones to remember this place as it was before it was destroyed.

Virago stopped one of them, placing her hand on his arm.

"Tell those who are already carrying things not to come back. We've run out of time."

The man nodded and then swam as quickly as he could to catch up with the small group that was already heading off.

"How are you going to find them all?" Alys asked, watching as they seemingly darted in countless directions. "No one is going to the same place."

"We always find each other." He didn't know how it was possible, but his people were good at coming back together. They would gather eventually. But for now, they all needed to get away from the metal demons in the distance.

His hearts squeezed as he looked at the billowing mass of dust and darkness behind the machines. They looked to be churning up the ground. Some of them were stuck at higher rises, but he could see they were eating away at the stone. Slowly digging themselves a flat plane. Anything in their way was destroyed. He could smell blood in the water, likely sea creatures who hadn't swum away from them fast enough.

"Brother," Virago said, her voice cutting through his horror. "We are needed."

"Of course."

He dragged Alys with him, although she hadn't said much yet. Then he dove into gathering whatever he could. He thrust everything he came in contact with into her arms. Tapestries, rugs, woven jewelry, whatever his hands found, he tossed to her.

"Whose are these?" she asked, looking down into the mass of items in her arms.

"I don't know," he muttered, looking around for more things to grab. "It doesn't matter right now. Once we're all back together, we'll figure out who owns what."

"You act like you've done this before."

"We have," he absentmindedly replied, gathering things in his own arms now that he realized she couldn't carry more. "Sometimes it's natural disasters, other times your people get too close and we move again. We cannot take the risk of them finding out about us."

"But they already know you exist."

He froze as he remembered that. "Right. I need to tell the others about that so we don't get too close on our scouting." Arms full, he rotated, so she was above him. "Can you hold on to me?"

Her delicate hand wrapped around his shoulder and she held on as he swam them far away from those chomping machines that destroyed so much of his world. Imber felt a bit like he was leaving behind a version of himself that he might not get back. There was so much he didn't know. So much he wanted answers to. But this place would not be where he gathered those answers. Not when he had so many people to take care of.

They moved a long distance away until he could smell some of his people gathered just on the edge of a drop off that disappeared into the abyss. He joined them there, his hearts aching. They all gathered together, tails twined as they watched their home disappear in the distance.

He dropped his armful of things and then turned to help Alys empty her arms as well. "We'll wait here until we cannot any longer."

"Why are they just going to watch?" she asked. Her face was redder than he remembered. "You're all going to stay here and just watch your home get torn apart?"

"We mourn for what we lost," he replied. "We will watch it because it should not die on its own. Just as we stay with those we love when it is their time. Nothing should disappear alone. Not even the place that holds so many memories for us."

Her hands twisted in her skirts and suddenly she turned to him with a determined expression. "I don't know those droids, but I think I can figure them out. I can dismantle them. If you get me close enough, then I can figure out how to stop them. We can freeze them in their tracks."

Something in him cracked. He trailed the back of his hand

down her cheek, loving her more than he ever had before. "They will just send more, Alys."

"Then we will keep shutting them down. It will be a graveyard of metal beats, I know, but you will still have your home."

"We do not wish to live in a graveyard."

"You have to do something!" she shouted, her voice carrying until all of his people stared at her. She turned to them, as though they would help her instead of him. "You can't just let them take your home. Not this easily. There are so many of you and those are just machines! I've seen Imber rip glass off my submarine. Surely there is something we can do."

He touched her shoulder, squeezing a little too hard. "Alys. We could fight until there are none of us left, but we have seen what your people are capable of. We know when we are outmatched."

She turned red rings eyes to him. "I cannot stand by and just let them do this."

"Breathe, little one. And let it go."

"It's my fight too," she snarled. "It's my fight because you are now my people. I can help. You have me now. It's not just your people who cannot fathom what mine have created. Those are just droids. They rely on wires and technology, which means there are parts of them that cannot be exposed to salt water. I can figure this out, Imber."

He wished it was that easy. He wished his people could return to a nest that had so much hardship but even now, looking at the destroyed landscape and all the black dust that already was at the edge of where they had lived and he knew... none of them would ever return to that haunted place.

"It's too late, Alys." He patted her shoulder a few times, trying to draw her back to this moment. "There are people here who need our help. We can help them. They are right in front of us, and we will not stop helping others simply because there is a fight that we may or may not win. Our home is lost. Now we look to the home we can build."

She let out a choked little sob. "I can't do that. I can't live with myself if I don't try, Imber."

Sighing, he let her spin away from him and lunge back to where they had come from. He could feel his hearts breaking, and the way his stomach rolled as she disconnected from him. No longer breathing for both of them, he took a deep breath into his lungs for the first time in a full day.

She had to feel it. She must have realized that she'd ripped herself free, and still she swam as though she could cross that distance without him.

Virago swam to his side, an amused expression on her face. "She's a feral little thing. What just happened?"

"She wants to go back and destroy her people's creations," he murmured. "She thinks she can stop them all."

"Then she is delusional as well as fierce. Sounds like someone I know." Virago slapped his back hard enough to rock him forward. "Go get your mate, brother. I'll gather the others while we can."

He swam after the short distance Alys had gone and then gathered her up in his arms. She slapped at him, even raked his skin with her tiny claws as she struggled to free herself. But by the time he'd connected them, forcing air through the tentacle and into her lungs, she'd lost all her fight.

Limp in his arms, he gathered her close to his hearts, pressed a kiss to her temple, and whispered into her hair, "It's gone, Alys. It's already gone."

CHAPTER
Thirteen

ALYS SURVEYED the devastation with a sense of detachment. It was almost like she wasn't here at all. Looking over what had once been a home, and she'd only gotten a small glimpse of it.

Had it ever really been here? Had she made it up in her head?

All the machines had left. The droids that were made to landscape and terraform had completed their job. And now, she came back with Imber and his people to see the decimation of what had once been a beautiful coil of nests.

The little stone patterns were gone. Just dust in their place. They couldn't even swim too close to the ground because all the dust left over from the machines was so fine that it would puff up and darken the water. So they stayed far above the home of the undines, even though she could see how badly they wanted to visit it. Even just to touch the ground with their hands, so they could feel connected to this place one last time.

Her heart broke for them. With them.

And when another undine appeared out of the foggy water, his face dirty and his hands shaking, she knew there was still more to grieve.

Imber held her tight to him as they sped through the water.

They fairly flew to another group of undines who had somehow gotten injured. She wasn't sure how or what had happened. It didn't matter in the end. They were injured. She had two good hands. If she could help, she would.

So she spent hours doing whatever it was that the undines needed. Alys patched people up who had scrapes or cuts. She smeared foul feeling liquid onto their wounds and held their hands while others stitched them together. She did whatever was required of her, because it was the only thing she could do.

Her people were the ones who had caused this. She felt like she owed them so much, even if all she had right now was her time.

Imber sat behind her, doing the same thing. Their backs touched often. He would reach behind him and gently trail his fingers over her hip sometimes, just to let her know he was still there. Still with her.

But it didn't help. Nothing she did helped.

No matter how many people she bandaged, patched, or just sat and held their hands, it didn't change what had happened. Their homes were gone. Their hopes were drenched underneath years of fear that her people had breathed into them.

Though not all of them knew she could understand them, she could. She listened to their fears and their worries. How they still hadn't found one of their dear friends who had fled. What if one of those metal creatures had gotten ahold of them? There was blood in the water. They could all smell it. Something had happened and now they couldn't put themselves back together.

Maybe it would change soon. Maybe these people were hardy and strong. They'd come out of this as better versions of themselves, having survived something difficult together.

But she looked at them and she thought... this was her fault.

"Alys?" Imber asked. His tail came around her like a giant snake, circling her entire body and pushing away those who had been close to her.

"What are you doing?" she asked as the other undine's hand

slid out of hers. She narrowed her gaze at the thick muscle suddenly banding around her waist. "Why are you circling me?"

He reached for her hands, lifting them and holding them in front of her eyes.

Her fingers were bleeding. Red bloomed in the weak light, and then his entire body lit up. Bright, sparkling points of green up and down his form. It only illuminated the blood even more.

All the help she'd given, every moment of her trying to make up for what her people had done, she hadn't realized she'd been risking herself so much. Staring down at her fingers now, she realized that she was going to die very soon if they didn't do something. Somehow, in all of this, Alys had forgotten that humans can't stay in the water for so long.

Her skin was wrinkled and pale, skin cracking on her palms, and then she suddenly realized there were far more effects of staying underwater this long. She hadn't noticed because she was so upset that it had been easy to ignore how badly her body hurt. Now, seeing herself injured, it hit her like a sledgehammer.

Her body ached, all of her muscles feeling tired in a way that they'd never felt before. She was so thirsty and had a headache blooming behind her eyes that had only happened once before when she'd gone too long without water. But this time it was so much more intense right between her eyes, like her brain was warning her about... something. Her stomach clenched in hunger, but she didn't know how long it had been since she'd eaten anything.

She didn't even realize that her body was listing to the side until Imber gently propped her up. He pulled her pale, wrinkled hands out of her eyesight. "What is happening to you?"

"I think the water..." Alys lifted her shaking hands again, just so she could see the damage. So it wasn't entirely made up in her own head. "I can't stay in the water this long. How long has it been?"

His concerned gaze focused on her hands before he cleared his throat. "I don't... I don't know."

"How many sunrises?"

"Three."

"How deep are we?"

He shook his head. "I don't know what that means. There is no measurement for me to give you."

She looked up at the surface, her mind ticking through all the possibilities. She didn't think she was deep enough to get the bends. It wasn't likely, anyway. What if all of this made her sick? What if going to the surface made her blood boil and her body just gave up?

"Slowly," she finally whispered. "I need to go to the surface very slowly. Just in case."

"Just in case what?"

With a wide-eyed stare, she hoped she conveyed how terrified she was. And to his credit, Imber didn't question her any more. He just gathered her in his arms and started their ascent.

They weren't that far down, come to find out. It only took them a few minutes to get to where she could see the surface clearly. But she could also see there wasn't any land anywhere near them.

"I need to get out of the water," she said. And everything in her hurt. She needed food. She needed fresh water. She needed...

Not to be here.

Her heart broke. She wanted to be with him and now, it was startlingly real that this might not be possible. They were creatures from two very different places in this world, and neither of them could change that.

He swam with her all the way to the surface, holding her head above the water so she didn't have to kick or swim. She was limp in his arms, allowing him to do all the work as she stared up at the cloudy sky.

Almost delirious, the only thing she could think to say was, "It looks like a storm is coming."

"There are always storms, Alys."

"This one looks worse than normal," she whispered, before turning her tear filled gaze to him. "I'm so sorry, Imber."

"Why are you apologizing?"

"Because I've only been down here a few days with you and I'm already breaking apart. I'm in pieces. I thought we could..."

Imber let out a little grumble before drawing her closer. He pressed their foreheads together, above the sea. The waves caressed her cheeks, and the air made her shiver, even though he lent her some small amount of warmth.

Gently, he pulled the cord out of her neck and held onto the back of her head with a fierce grip. "You and I were meant for each other, my wave song. That doesn't mean this will be easy, or that we will not have to fight for each other. But we will be fine, Alys. You and I are more than the sea and the sky. Will we fight through this, just as we have fought through everything. Now, tell me what you need."

She didn't want to tell him what she needed because it meant they would be parted. She didn't know if they would ever see each other again if she did what she knew had to be done.

"I need to go back," she whispered, her voice breaking on the words. "I'm so sorry."

"Back?" he asked, his eyes searching hers. But then he blew out a long breath and nodded. "Because you can't survive very long under the ocean, can you?"

"I can't survive in water for so long." She didn't want to disappoint him. She didn't want to disappoint herself, but everything was so clear. "I have to see my father. Maybe..."

They both stared at each other and she knew he was thinking the same thing as her. Her father wasn't the safest person for her to go, but there was no one that was safe.

Sighing, Imber nodded. "I trust you. Wherever you need me to take you, I will bring you there. And we will continue on as we always have. You and I were meant to be together. I have no fear that we will not find each other again after this."

Grabbing onto his face with her worn and torn hands, she

squeezed as hard as she could so he would know she was seri-ous. "I will come back to you, Imber. There is nothing on this planet that can stop me. I will be back, and I will come home. Do you hear me?"

"Home?"

"You are my home." She leaned forward and pressed her lips to his, wondering if even her face wasn't the same as it had been before. "You will always be my home."

Words pressed against her lips. Words that would bind her to him far more than anything else she'd ever said before.

Did she say it? Did she tell him how she really felt when he hadn't said the same? She'd never been the first person to admit feelings in a relationship, but then again, this could very well be the last time she'd ever seen him.

So with no one but him to hear her, with the waves crashing around their shoulders, she said bright and clear, "I love you, Imber. More than I can really say. You have changed my life for the better and I refuse to go back to how it was before. I'd rather die. Without you at my side, the world is colorless and bleak. I don't know if you feel the same way, but I don't think I really care either way. You are everything I have ever wanted."

He smiled at her, then pressed a kiss to her palm before swimming them toward what she could only assume was her old home. "Haven't you been listening, Alys? I've called you my mate more times than I can count. I chose you for life, whether you will have me or not. I am yours, my wave song. All yours to do with as you wish, and that will never change."

With that thought warming her heart, she laid back and let him do all the work. He kept them both above the water so she could get some fresh air, but she also wondered if it was because he wanted to slow them down. If he didn't rush through the water toward her people, then he could hold her a little longer. What were a few more moments when it came to the end they feared?

Still, they reached her old home far too soon. She could sense it. Even though her eyes were turned up toward the sky, she knew the moment he tensed underneath her back that they were close. Even his clawed hands flexed on her waist, as though he wouldn't let go of her after all.

Alys knew the turmoil that ran through his mind. There was so much he wanted to say. Or perhaps that he wanted to do. His people were fighters, and his hands tightened around her waist. Perhaps he was thinking of keeping her, and not let her return.

But if he kept her, then he was the one hurting her. It was a struggle he did not know how to win. Unfortunately, she didn't think there was any winning in this situation.

"Here we are, wave song." The nickname shifted into one that warmed her cold bones. It made almost everything all right as he turned her in his arms and pressed their foreheads together again. "Come back to me."

"Always."

"You promise?"

She took a deep breath. "I more than promise. I vow to you, here and now, that I will not leave you for any longer than I have to. I will come to our home and I will figure out a way to fix this. I love you, Imber, and I will not be parted from you any longer than is necessary."

He nodded, seeming to understand that she needed him to know that she was telling the truth. Every ounce of her being wanted to be with him, and she suspected it was the same for him.

He took them underneath one of the docks, the one nearest to her home. She didn't ask how he knew where she lived. It just seemed right that he did.

There was a small ladder underneath the dock near her home. Her father had put it there just in case one of the submarines ran out of fuel and had to be serviced close to them. It took every ounce of her energy to put her hands on the rungs and pull herself up. Hand by hand. Movement by movement. By the time she got onto the dock, she wanted to lie down on it and catch her breath. But she also knew that Imber was watching her.

Anyone could be watching her. The last thing she needed was the General or his men realizing that she had come home with one of the undines. They would take him. Exploit him.

Or perhaps they would just kill him. Without questioning why or how he was at their home, they might just shoot him on sight.

So she rolled onto her hands and knees, breathing so hard she could taste metal in her mouth. But she still poked her head over the edge and attempted a smile down at him. "I'm all right," she said. "I'll be back soon. I will find you, Imber."

He pressed his hand to his heart and then reached the webbed fingers out to her. "My heart is yours, Alys. Take good care of it."

And then he sank beneath the waves as she forced herself to her feet and staggered toward her home. There was a side door she could slip into if she was careful and quiet.

Then maybe she could find her father.

CHAPTER

Fourteen

EVERYTHING WAS A WHIRLWIND AFTER THAT. Imber watched from below the dock as she slipped into the house and there was very little he could see from the water. But her father was a sneaky man, far more than his daughter likely realized. Imber could watch him far easier than he could his mate.

The professor had built himself more than just the one facility to keep all the items from Imber's people. His sister had come here to investigate after he'd told her what Alys had told him. It didn't take very long for them to put two and two together.

Obviously, Alys's father hadn't told her everything.

Which meant it was up to him and his people to find out the whole truth about what this man didn't want Alys to see. Easily enough, really, because her father had built himself a tank underneath the ocean to sit in.

Or something like that. Virago had only explained it in simple terms, and he thought it was long pastime for him to see it himself. It wasn't hidden, not really. Alys had never swum near their home or she would have seen it. Anyone could see it.

Her father had added another level underneath their home, and the majority of it was glass. Imber could see right through the walls and track every step the professor made. Though the man was deep in thought, he really should look up at the glass more often. If he had, then he would see Imber floating right beyond it.

Alys had said her people were dangerous. She told him about the many risks and how nervous she was about all of it. In some sense, he knew there was logic to her fear. He had seen what their machines had done to his home and how those creations had eaten up rock and mountains of land that stood in their way. He knew there were likely other creations they had made as well.

But if he were to meet one alone, without any of their metal warriors, Imber had no question he was the stronger creature.

So he stayed where he was. Unafraid that her father would see him on the other side of the glass, watching him. If he was being honest with himself, he wanted the old man to see him. To feel the fear that surely he should feel.

Eventually, however, he got nervous. Alys had gone into the home a while ago and still her father was down here. The old man surely could hear her upstairs, or at the very least, she had to be shouting for him.

His mate needed help. And this was the only person who could give her that help.

Angry now, he slapped his fluke against the glass. Hard. That made the old man jump high enough that all the papers in his hands were flung into the air. They fell like the ash and dust that remained of his home before the man realized there was someone outside his window. Someone who was much larger and significantly more dangerous.

Imber bared his teeth in a pleased grin as he watched all the blood drain from the old man's face. Fear flickered in his movements, and he looked over at the door before looking back at Imber. As though he thought the monster at his windows was about to break in and flood the entire place.

But Imber did not want to harm the old man. Not yet.

Instead, he pressed a finger to his lips, as Alys had done to him once when he was talking too much, and then pointed up.

The professor clearly had no idea what that meant. Somehow his face turned even paler, like the inside of a clam shell. What a shame, really, because Imber enjoyed seeing the sun-kissed burnish of the achromo's skin.

Again, he pointed up, then gestured for the old man to leave.

That seemed to get the professor moving, because he bolted from the room like it was about to implode at any minute. Rolling his eyes, Imber made sure he was tucked away and out of sight from anyone above the water.

He should return home. He should go back to his people and make sure they were well. But he couldn't leave. Not yet, at least. He had to make sure that Alys was getting treated for whatever ailment bothered her, and then he could return to his people.

All he knew was that it felt as though he'd ripped out his heart when she walked away from him. He had seen the way she stumbled, the way pain had been laced in every single step, and he'd known in that moment he couldn't leave.

Not yet.

Soon, he would convince himself that she was in good hands.

He had no idea how long he waited. Coiled around the base of the building, he could have been there for days on end. Likely was, considering how stiff his tail was. Eventually, though, he peeled himself away from the cold stone and looked through the glass.

There was a sound there, and one that he'd been waiting to hear.

The clipped footsteps coming down the stairs were too many to just be one person. Which meant the professor was returning with another person at his side. Imber knew he should dart away from the glass and hide. Who knew who the professor was bringing? The other person could easily be someone who was meant to fight against Imber, to attack him or burn him as they had his people before.

It was a risk he was willing to take. Just in case the person on the other side of the glass was... was...

Alys came down the stairs and filled the room like a ray of sunshine. Her golden hair had been washed and brushed, and he could see it was just as beautiful as it had been when he'd first seen her. Those locks were shiny and smooth, falling around her head in a cascade of golden curls like a waterfall. Her skin was nearly back to normal, although there were still a few red lines at her joints that clearly hadn't healed just yet. But the dark circles under her lovely eyes were gone, and the bright expression on her face was full of life.

Just as he would always remember her. Because this was how she looked the first time he'd met her, and it was that first glimpse that had filled his soul with sunlight.

She was so beautiful that it was hard to breathe when he looked at her.

And her? She bolted toward the glass the moment she saw him. Ran for him, moving faster than he'd realized her kind could until she was right there. So close he could have touched her if there wasn't a barrier between them.

Just like the first time they'd seen each other, she lifted her hand and pressed it against the glass. So he mirrored her, wishing he could actually touch her.

He wanted to hold her and make sure that she was still really alive. He wanted to feel her against his chest, to know without a doubt, she wasn't broken. She wasn't still injured.

Though she still looked a little tired, she was now with him. He thought perhaps it had been days on end that he'd been here. His people must be wondering where he was, but he...

It didn't matter. He was with his mate.

All of his gills flared wide, and he knew his tail was already lighting up. He took a risk that someone might see him, but he wanted her to know without words that he was happy to see her.

He wanted her to know that he'd waited for her. And he would continue to wait until the very end of time if that was what it took.

Her father stood awkwardly behind her. Though there was a muffled quality to their voices, Imber could still make out what they were saying.

"So this is him?" her father asked.

"This is Imber, Dad."

"Imber," her father repeated, as though trying to press the name into memory. Then he did something that Imber didn't expect. The professor walked right up to the glass and cleared his throat. "We haven't been officially introduced, but hello. My name is Jasper Fairweather, and I've heard quite a bit about you."

He blinked at the old man, surprised that he was so bold when the last time he'd seen him, the man had run up the stairs, tripping as he went. "Any family of Alys's is family of mine. If they're brave enough."

Alys eyed him before repeating the words to her father, word for word. Even the last bit that he had intended to be nothing more than intimidation.

Jasper swallowed hard, his throat working before he nodded. "It's not as easy as you make it sound, I'm afraid. There are more people at risk here than just you or I. I'm sure you know about the city we intend to build."

"My home was destroyed, old man. I think we know your people are out to kill mine."

Again, Alys repeated it, although she gave him a glare before adding on, "We were there when the droids started clearing and flattening for Alpha. His people were living there, Dad. More than that, there were some of his people who were injured. It's not right what is happening."

"I already told you I cannot stop it." Her father staggered over to a large box covered in paper and sat down behind it. "There is little I can do. I could sabotage the architectural plans, but all that would succeed in doing is murdering countless people. The city would implode, and their home would still be gone. But on top of it, there would be hundreds, if not thousands, of our own people dead."

"You shouldn't have designed it in the first place," Alys hissed.

"I know." Her father looked first at her, then at Imber on the other side of the glass. His gaze lingered where their hands were still pressed together, his voice shaking as he replied. "I know there was so much I could have done differently. It's why I'm not suggesting that I go back with you. My darling, there is nothing I can do now. I have to go down with my own ship."

"You aren't a captain, Dad."

"No, but I am the person who created the destruction. I'm not going to ask him or his people to forgive me. I have done something that is unforgivable." Her father leaned forward, his fingertips pressed together against his lips. "But perhaps there is still something I can do for my daughter. The only person I have ever really loved."

Silence fell then.

Imber wanted to ask what the old man was talking about. How could he help Alys? The ocean would forever wear at her body, and though he suspected there was some form of magic to what the achromos did, he didn't think it was possible to change her body into something else.

Alys let her hand slip from the glass as she turned to her father. "What do you mean?"

"You cannot stay here." The old man looked defeated as he said it. "The General has already heard about your sub returning, ripped apart and without its pilot. There are too many variables at your return, and the man is already ridiculously suspicious about your friends coming and ruining his new city. You cannot be here. No one can know that you are."

"I know that," Alys replied, taking a step closer to her father. "I just didn't know where else to go."

"You need somewhere safe to live."

Of that, he agreed. Imber swam to the window closer to her father, a little farther from Alys. "I agree with that. The ocean will kill her, old man. So what are you suggesting?"

Alys made a grumpy noise at him and then did not translate what he had just said. "Dad, I tried to live with him under the water. You, of all people, know what the ocean can do to our bodies. It's just not possible for me to live there."

"And you cannot live above the ocean either."

Imber frowned, his eyes darting from achromos to achromos before growling, "And why is that?"

This time she translated for him, and Jasper turned to give him a look that clearly said her father wasn't pleased with his daughter's chosen mate. "We are all going under the sea for a reason, undine. There are many risks to staying above the water now. Our world is slowly dying. Between the storms, the volcanoes, the plagues, all of it. It's sweeping across this world and there is nothing we can do to stop it. The only thing we can do now is to hide."

"Then hide above the water," he growled.

Jasper looked to his daughter for translation, then sighed. "I wish it were possible. There is nowhere left for us to hide. I could build my daughter a small home here in a few months, but within a year, it would be destroyed. For her to safely stay in touch with you, it has to be near the sea. And if it is near the sea, then the storms will rip it apart. She would die. Do you understand that? Above the sea, there is nowhere for her to safely live. And there is nowhere for us to go other than under the waves."

So that was the problem. Her people were dying out, and they were fleeing in whatever direction they could to stay alive.

It posed a problem. Because he did not want to kill any species without cause, but he also did not want to share his home. Not with so many creatures who had no sense about them.

He grunted in understanding and then said, "Then you must bring the air to her."

Alys translated, and her father nodded. "My thoughts exactly, undine. We will bring the air to her and that will be my parting gift to my daughter. A love letter made of metal and all the parts that will be needed to keep her alive into old age. Perhaps beyond. I have hope that maybe someday, our kind will see to reason that there is more we can give each other than battle and war."

Imber did not share the same hope. Namely, because he didn't believe it was possible.

Their kinds were designed to fight each other. To battle until the bitter end, until there was nothing left in the ocean but blood and salt.

Still, he nodded for the old man's sake, and for Alys's.

"Dad," she whispered, and he saw that Alys's face had paled as well. "What are you planning on doing?"

"I'm going to build you a home, my dear. An escape pod unlike anything else." Her father seemed even more tired as he said the words. "But it will take time. Time that you need to stay here, hidden, so no one knows what I'm going to do. And then, at the last moment, I will set you free."

It made Imber's stomach roll, but he knew it was the best decision. So he swam closer to the window again, waiting for his mate to put her palm to the glass. "I will find you," he said to her. This time, he made the promise. "And soon, my love, my mate, you will be home again."

HER FATHER WORKED AS QUICKLY as he could. All the replicators were firing constantly, so much so that she could smell the molten metal most days. It still took months. Months on end while she hid in his home and pretended that she wasn't listening to all the builders who came and went. That she didn't care when they spoke about the progress they had made on Alpha.

Eventually, even she had to admit they had built something grand. An entire city encased in glass that would never leak. It was impossible to damage what her father had created. Three different bubbles, all encircling the city. If one was damaged, it was easy to fix without endangering the city. And even if they didn't know how to fix it, there were still three shields between them and the world.

The oxygen remained stable. Everything grew quite well underneath the natural sunlight and also all the UV bulbs that they had throughout the entire encasement. Even on cloudy days, Alpha saw the sun.

They rushed the next project, already having her father working night and day on yet another iteration. This time, it would be Beta. The city that was made like skyscrapers, all exposed to the ocean. They wanted a city to put the riff raff. The people who would fix everything they needed, the blue-collar workers who didn't need to be with the people who had already built Alpha.

In less than a few months, they created a new world and segregated everyone within it.

Her father worked so hard. First to make her a home so she didn't have to live with his mistakes, and then for his people to have somewhere safe to go after Alpha decided they were no longer necessary.

He lived, ate, and breathed work. Sometimes she went into his secret office in the water, trying to get him to eat something. But he didn't often eat.

Most of the time, he spent his minimal hours enacting his promise to his daughter. She didn't know if that was because he loved her so much, or if he felt guilty for what he had done.

There were only so many hours in the day, though. And his guilt ate at him.

Eventually, he finished. He came into her room late at night, like a ghost of himself. Pale and staggering, he braced himself on the frame of her bedroom door and nodded. "It is done."

"I will start packing."

"Everything you need is already in there," her father said, his voice crackling with age and exhaustion. "You have to go now."

Alys stood, clutching her shawl around herself. She was in nothing but her white nightgown with a pale yellow shawl to keep her warm before bed. He really expected her to leave like this?

"Why?" she asked, furrowing her brows in confusion. "What is going on?"

"They're coming to help pack the house. They want me working in Alpha from now on." He looked around the room, then grabbed a photograph of her mother, her father, and Alys. "Keep this, at least. The rest you can leave."

"Dad, I don't know what's going on."

"You have to go, now. They're going to be here very soon, and they will see what I have built. There's no time for us to talk, Alys." He drew her in for a tight hug, his chin on top of her head and then the briefest press of a kiss to her skull. "I will miss you, my girl. But maybe there will be a way for us to send messages to each other. You never know."

"I'll try my best." She squeezed him tight as well, trying to press into him how much she appreciated all his work and how much she would miss him, too. For all that he had done, he was still her dad. And he still had done his best to make sure that he not only got her out of this place, but that she was happy and where she wanted to be.

The future waited for her. Soon she would see Imber again, and all the creatures that had made her fall in love with the sea. She would live and breathe with them, even if her life would be a little different than before.

She'd thought she would be elated at this moment, but there was a bittersweet sadness to it.

"I love you," she whispered against her father's shoulder. "I really do, you know?"

"I always know." He drew back and framed her face with his hands. Holding onto her as he looked. Just looked. Like he didn't want to forget the sight of her face and it made tears sting in her eyes. "Just like you will always know that I love you, my daughter. The best thing I have ever made was you. And will always be you."

A single tear dripped down her cheek before they both burst into movement. She held the photo tightly as they sprinted out of the house toward the abandoned dock where her father had been building. No one came over here. No one ever even looked at their house, really, but they needed to make sure she was gone long before anyone else came.

Opening the top hatch, she clambered in before sticking her head out. "Dad!"

He looked back at her, an old man standing on an old dock,

his shoulders curved and his body weighed down by time. "What is it?"

"How will I find them?" Neither of them had seen Imber or any undine in months. Not since the last time she'd seen him.

Her father grinned. "I think he'll find you."

She wasn't sure how he was so certain of that, but... Well, she wasn't going to question it. Alys slipped into the pilot station at the head of the massive ship he had built her. And really, it wasn't a ship at all. It was a home.

She hadn't gotten to explore the entire thing, but soon she would. And then she would be free. Really free.

Firing up the engines, she turned her new home away from the old one and set off into the sea. Alys didn't know where she was going or how far she would need to travel to find him and the others. So she just... explored.

For weeks on end. Piloting her ship through all parts of the ocean she had never seen before. Endless darkness below her, wild creatures like whales and sharks and jellyfish that didn't care when she moved through their masses. She saw perfect, glistening white sand, and so many forests of kelp and greenery that it seemed like they turned into emeralds in front of her eyes. So many creatures and plants that she'd never seen before. And she cataloged it all.

She spent most of her time cataloging all the things she found while she traveled. Alys had always wanted to have free rein of the sea and to go wherever she wanted. But she'd never thought it would come in the form of a pod that was her home as well.

Her father had done a miraculous job. It was large enough for her to walk from end to end most days around thirty times and feel a bit like she was getting some form of exercise. There was a bathroom with a small shower that filtered the salt out of the sea. The central area was mostly taken up by a large moon pool, but she rarely opened that, anyway. So it felt like there was a big empty space in the middle with three branches off of it.

The first branch had small stairs that went up to the bedroom with a glass dome over her mattress. She'd already started painting a mural around it, so it felt like she was sleeping in a bed of flowers.

The second branch went to her piloting area, which was mostly functional with many panels, buttons, and gadgets.

The last went to a massive garden. Or a greenhouse, she supposed. It also had a large glass dome surrounding it, so the plants got as much natural light as they were allowed. The rest of the UV light the pod provided. Already she had a ridiculous amount of food available, and she'd been spending her evenings canning vegetables and fruits, while also learning the fine art of drying herbs for flavor.

Who would have thought propagating plants was so interesting? But she found her new life to be thoroughly thrilling. She was the only one who could keep herself alive, and strangely, she had risen to that challenge with vigor and hope.

Of course, that hope wavered slightly the longer it took for him to find her, but... She was still holding on.

Tucking herself in at night was the hardest part. She settled in, pulling the down blankets up over her shoulders and staring up at the stars. She'd parked herself on a small rise tonight, a swimmable distance to the surface. For some reason, she really wanted to see the stars.

Tonight felt like she needed it. And it was a clear night, so why wouldn't she see the beauty of the sky above her?

But this time, a dark shadow passed over the stars as she looked up at it. A shadow that wasn't quite right for any of the whales and dolphins she'd seen before. It was... different.

Sitting straight up, her hair tumbling around her shoulders, she held her breath as the shadow got closer and closer.

"Imber," she whispered at the same time the dark night sea lit up with a thousand sparkling emeralds.

Bolting out of bed, she got tangled up in the sheets and fell straight onto her face as she raced for the moon pool. Untangling herself as best she could, she dragged half of her bedding with her before she could slam her hand down on the level that opened the moon pool.

"Come on," she muttered, jumping up and down as she waited. "Hurry up. Hurry up."

She didn't even think it might be another undine. She knew Imber. And her soul knew him, too.

The moment there was enough space for him to slip into the room, he was there. His dark head cresting the water and a wicked grin on his face that made every fiber of her being light on fire.

He stayed there, floating in the water with his hair plastered against his head, looking like a sea god waiting for her. That grin never budged, and his eyes never moved from her. "Alys," he said, that deep voice sending shivers down her spine. "You finally came home."

With an ear-piercing shriek, she launched herself into the water. Right into his waiting arms. His laughter echoed through her room, but she didn't want to hear him laughing. She wanted to kiss him.

So she wrapped her arms around his shoulders and did just that. She kissed him with all the desire and waiting that she'd felt for months. It had been such a long time since she'd seen him, and it didn't matter if he had found someone else or he'd moved on from her. She didn't want to know.

Not yet, anyway. Right now, she just wanted to feel his soft lips against hers. To feel the bite of his sharp teeth and the strange sensation of his bumpy tongue against hers. She wanted him more than she'd ever wanted anything and she would have him.

His arms tightened around her and he kissed her like he'd been counting every single day until he could kiss her again. Maybe he had. It certainly felt that way as he pressed months of despair and hope and agony against her tongue.

She had no idea how long they kissed. All she knew was that they could take as much time as they needed.

For the first time since knowing him, there was no clock. No time for them to keep track of. No reason to hurry. They could explore each other, love each other, in every way, shape, and form. It didn't matter.

There was no one waiting for them this time. It was just the two of them.

And so, when she felt the prick at the side of her neck as he drifted with her under the water, she didn't stop him. Her nightgown floated up around her waist and that was okay, too. She didn't need it. He would keep her safe, and right now, she wasn't all that worried about safety in the slightest.

She wanted him. He wanted her. And it had been months since they had last explored each other's bodies.

There was no rush in any of their touches. Just long sighs and deep breaths as they relearned every inch of the other's body. Imber had new scars, a few on his shoulders and one rather large one across his abs. She had gained a few pounds, but he didn't seem to mind in the slightest.

And when he sank inside her, she felt her soul heal from all the times they'd been apart. She had missed him. So much. Now they were together, and it was overwhelming how happy she was.

Eventually he swam her back up to the moon pool, his arms still tightly wrapped around her as he set her on the edge.

He stayed between her parted legs, his hands on her face as he traced all the parts of her that he loved. His fingers lingered on her lips, her cheeks, her collarbone, like he couldn't stop touching her.

"Alys," he said again, his voice little more than a low murmur. "I have missed you so, my wave song."

"I missed you, too." She caught his hand to press a kiss to his palm. "How is everything?"

"We have a new home. There are more people who have come with us, others displaced by the work of the achromos. But soon it will be done, and we will be safe again."

"I'm glad to hear it. I cannot leave this ship as often as I'd like, but I can visit with you. Visit them, if they'll have me."

"I think they're happy on their own, love." His eyes seemed a little distant, sadness bleeding into his gaze before he shook it free. "It would be best if it was just you and I."

Though it made her sad, she understood. The undines had their own way of life and her people hadn't made that way of life any easier. It was hard, but it was the right choice.

Nodding, she toyed with the ends of his hair. "Will that make you happy? I don't want to isolate you."

"Oh, you are my love, my mate, my everything," he breathed. "I would not survive being parted from you again, Alys. Not even in death."

When she drew him in for another kiss, Alys knew that maybe he was right. Maybe they were meant to be together forever. It certainly felt that way. But no matter what, their life would always be an adventure.

And there was no one she would rather adventure with than him.

Epilogue

ALYS REACHED OVERHEAD, her body straining to get ahold of the grape tomatoes she'd been growing. They were a finicky bunch. Usually plants grew quite well in her underwater home, but the sky had been much more angry these days. Soon enough, she might have to reprogram the ship to move.

The sun was blotted out of the sky by storms these days. Not even ash. It was like there was a never ending wall of clouds and she only had so many grow lights in this place. It was safe, still. At least that much she knew. She could live here for her entire lifetime, and the home her father had built her would keep her alive.

If she did her part.

Finally grabbing the bunch of tomatoes, she brought them down onto the table and started cutting. Today was a special day, after all.

Twenty years. She'd been under the water with him for twenty years and she wanted to do something special for the undine who had filled her heart with so much joy.

Rushing now, she got the salad prepared and brought it out into the main living area. So much had changed since her first day here. She'd painted the walls numerous times. For now, she'd settled on sunflowers. Tomorrow, she might change her mind and bring waves back inside like she had before. The sheets were far more threadbare, but they were worn in and more comfortable than they used to be. The metal was rusted along the edges of the moon pool. She frowned at that and told herself that she'd clean them up once she got the chance.

Alys had laid out a blanket next to the water and piled it high with all the food she could. Of course, most of it was vegetables from her expansive garden. But there was plenty of that to go around, and she wanted him to try some of the summer squash she'd been growing. She even baked it this time, since sauteed squash had been "offensive" the last time he'd tried it.

Besides, she had two platters of fish ready for them. One for her, cooked and seasoned with a heavy amount of basil on top. His raw, with every bone picked clean, so he didn't have to worry about stabbing himself.

Everything was ready.

She waited until the water stirred, just a bit. Enough so that she could see that beloved head crest the surface and the bright grin on his face. Imber was just as handsome as he'd been twenty years ago.

"You," she said with a laugh as he rose the rest of the way out of the water. "What have you brought me?"

Imber's arms were full of sea flowers. He knew she couldn't have them out of the water, but he liked to dot them over the glass surface of her bedroom so every time she looked up, her vision was full of rainbow colors.

"Happy anniversary, wave song," he said.

She shook her head, but then nodded for him to head up. "Go on, then. I'll wait."

Imber ducked underneath the water and arced over her home. She watched that massive, emerald green tail flickering above her head with all the sparks of green light as he showered flowers down upon her. Some of the petals broke off, looking like falling leaves that she remembered seeing in her youth.

A rare beam of sunlight broke through the clouds, illuminating the handsome undine who had stolen her heart.

He returned, looking quite pleased with himself. "What have you gotten for me?"

Spreading her arms wide, she gestured to everything laid out in front of them. "A feast for my mate."

Already he was licking his lips, like he hadn't tried food like this countless times before. He was always so sweet to her, though. Since the first moment they met.

Together, they fell into the easy habit of eating together. He told her about his day, she told him about hers. Of course, Imber tended to experience more adventures. He had been talking with some of the other groups of undine who were closer to the surface.

"The waveriders were pleased to see the last of the humans were swept out to sea." He took a deep breath, holding it for a long time before he allowed himself to exhale. "I fear there are none of your people left on the surface, Alys."

"We knew it was coming. I just didn't think it would take this long for the ones who didn't get to the cities to..." She couldn't say the words.

"Enough dark talk. What did you do today, my love?"

The soft expression on his face soothed her to the core. "I've been working in the garden more. Oh, and your sister stopped by with your niece."

"They aren't supposed to do that," he grumbled.

"They don't like it that I'm alone in here. Neither do you."

He huffed out a breath. "I'm just trying to keep you all safe. If anyone else found out--"

She reached for his hand, holding it against her lips as she kissed his salty knuckles. "No one will find out, Imber. They're very careful to wash themselves of my scent, and besides, no one comes out here. We're all perfectly safe."

He reached for her, brushing the back of his claw against her cheek. For a moment, everything seemed to stand still. They just looked at each. Both of them seeing the only person who they would give up the world for.

"You are as beautiful as the first day I met you," he murmured, that claw trailing down to her jaw. "More beautiful, in fact. I didn't know that was possible."

She leaned into him. "You are much larger than the day I met you."

"The People of Water never stop growing." He looked pleased with the assessment, though. "Are you ready for the second part of your anniversary gift?"

Alys looked over at the food they had demolished and wondered what else he would get her. "Did you find a new wreckage?"

"No."

She frowned, watching as he prowled closer to her. His tail slid out of the water, wet drops splattering all over her clean floor. "Did you discover some new species of fish you want to show me?"

"No."

How could she not know what had brought her? After all these years, she knew that look in his eye and that proud grin on his face when he was about to turn her world upside down and inside out in the best way possible.

He dragged his hand up her side, the webs catching on the fabric of her shirt.

"You still want me after all these years?" she asked, her voice a low murmur.

"Every wrinkle, every scar, every sign of your age is a testament to how much I love you," he murmured before kissing her and stealing all the breath from her lungs. "There is nothing on your body that will ever make me love you less. You are the light of my life, Alys. I am just lucky you saw use in me."

"Use?" Alys dragged her hands up his muscular chest, feeling the power there that had built for countless years now. "There is more to you than just use, my love. You have guided me through so much of my life and I am so lucky to have you as my partner."

"Happy anniversary. You and I are going to live through so many more of these."

"Are we now?"

"I couldn't imagine a life without you, Alys. And someday, when you decide your body is tired and your will to live has ended, I will hold your hand into the darkness." He kissed her soundly one more time and then grinned. "Now, no more talk of death. I want to live with you, wave song. Until the end of all things."

If you've found yourself here without reading the Deep Waters series first, that's totally fine! But you should know there is a deep world (pun intended) outside of just this novella! You can find that in the rest of the books here -

Whispers of the Deep